ALLAPATTAH

Novels by Patrick Smith

ALLAPATTAH
ANGEL CITY
THE BEGINNING
FOREVER ISLAND
A LAND REMEMBERED
THE RIVER IS HOME

ALLAPATTAH

Patrick Smith

Pineapple Press, Inc.
Sarasota, Florida

Inquiries should be addressed to:

Pineapple Press, Inc.
P.O. Box 3889
Sarasota, Florida 34230

www.pineapplepress.com

Library of Congress Cataloging-in-Publication Data

Smith, Patrick D., 1927-
  Allapattah / Patrick D. Smith.
    p. cm.
  ISBN 978-1-56164-565-7 (pbk. : alk. paper)
  1. Seminole Indians--Fiction. 2. Crocodiles--Fiction. 3. Human-animal relationships--Fiction. 4. Whites--Relations with Indians--Fiction. 5. Everglades (Fla.)--Fiction. I. Title.
  PS3569.M53785A79 2012
  813'.54--dc23
                                        2012026328

ISBN 978-0-910923-42-2 (hardback)
ISBN 978-1-56164-542-8 (e-book)

First Edition
10 9 8 7 6 5 4 3 2 1

Printed in the United States of America

Cover illustration by Stefan Martin
Cover design adapted from the jacket design by Frank Cochrane

ALLAPATTAH

ONE

A glowing orange dawn was invading the swamp when Toby Tiger walked across the small clearing and approached the chickee hut. Thin wisps of fog were clinging to tree limbs like blobs of cotton candy, and a light dew created puffy little beads in the limestone dust. Birds were moving now, and several chickens ventured into the edge of the woods in search of food. When one grabbed a small green snake and ran, others followed, cackling loudly.

Toby's wife, Lucy, was at an iron grill beneath the chickee, finishing a breakfast of grits, salt bacon and corn dodgers. She handed Toby a plate and then took one for herself.

They sat at a table beside the chickee and ate in silence, and then Lucy said, "Will you be gone all day?"

"I'll go by Allapattah Flats first and then to Grandfather's hammock. I should be back shortly after noon."

Lucy said, "I wish you wouldn't go to Allapattah Flats just to stare at those crocodiles. They're dangerous, and could do you great harm. You're the only Seminole man I've ever known who would go so far just to visit crocodiles."

"That's because before you married me you knew

only reservation Indians," Toby said, "and I'm one of the wild ones from the swamp. There's a great difference. And besides that, the crocodiles will leave me alone if I leave them alone. I don't bother them when I go there. I only look."

"I still wish you wouldn't go, but I know you will," Lucy said, resigned. "I don't understand what pleasure anyone gets from looking at such ugly creatures." She then changed the subject. "Please give my love to your grandfather. I wish he would come and live with us. He's too old to be out there in the Everglades alone, and I worry about his safety."

"I'll speak to him about this again, but I don't think he will listen. He's a stubborn old man and will do only as he wishes."

As soon as he finished eating, Toby took a bag from the table and entered a narrow trail leading into the swamp. Darkness almost came again as he walked beneath thick growths of pond cypress and cabbage palms and palmetto interlaced with vines. Bordering the trail there were lush beds of ferns, and in places the ground was covered solidly with green moss. Squirrels barked at him as Toby walked slowly and carefully to avoid snakes.

After a mile the woods became thinner, and here the path led across an open area of meadow dotted with cypress. In normal times this ground would have been soggy with a thin covering of water, but now the earth cracked beneath Toby's footsteps.

Soon he came to the bank of Lost Creek, a narrow black stream bordered thickly with willow and button brush. An airboat was partially hidden in a clump of pickerel weeds. Toby put the bag into the boat, shoved it away from the bank, and inserted the key. When he hit the starter, the airplane engine mounted on the rear of the boat thundered to life.

Toby had purchased the boat three years ago for the low price of $300 because the engine pistons were cracked. He had rebuilt the engine himself, and now the old boat would make a top speed of forty miles per hour. It was his most valued possession and his only means of getting around the Glades quickly. Before he had purchased the boat he made his weekly trip to his grandfather's hammock in an ancient cypress dugout canoe which still rested on the creek bank.

He guided the boat slowly along the winding stream, watching for signs of bass and turtles. Huge herons and snowy egrets, frightened by the roar, flapped away as he moved past them. Soon the stream blended into endless sawgrass, forming the vast Pa-Hay-Okee, the River of Grass flowing southward through the Florida Everglades to a point where marsh meets sea at Florida Bay.

For a few hundred yards Toby continued to drive the boat slowly, and then he rammed the throttle full forward. Staccato bursts of thunder roared from the engine, and the boat sprang forward like a horse stung by a hornet. Toby's eyes widened as he sat on the elevated driver's seat and skimmed along the top of the water, crashing through the solid wall of sawgrass as if it were not there at all. This was what he loved most, running wild with the wind, racing forward across the marsh as if nothing could block his way.

He turned westward, continuing to run the airboat at top speed. The open marsh was dotted with hammocks, which were islands covered with cabbage palms and lancewood and clumps of palmetto. Some were very small and some large, and occasionally he circled one, causing waves to rush into the bushes lining the shore. Gradually he came into an area of mangrove islands, the inner reaches of the Ten Thousand Islands. Here the water was brackish. Soon he slowed the boat as he approached an elevated island known as Allapattah Flats.

Toby moved slowly until he came to a cove leading inward, then he rammed the bow of the boat onto the shore and stepped out. He made his way carefully along a narrow path until he reached a point where the cove ended. On a bank on the opposite side of the cove, two huge crocodiles lay motionless, their jaws open wide and their eyes closed.

Toby looked across the cove, and then he squatted on his haunches and said, "Allapattah. Old long snouts. You may be called allapattah by some, but your real meaning is death. You would like to eat me, heh? You would kill all you touch, like instant death. But in the end you'll die too. You'll see. Only four of you are left, and someday soon there will be none. They will kill you, just as they are killing me, and there's nothing for both of us but death."

For several minutes more Toby watched the crocodiles, then he picked up a stick and threw it into the water. When the crocodiles hissed menacingly, he said, "That's not me in the water, only a stick. If I jump into a pond with the alligator, he'll leave and go into another pond, but if I jump in there with you, you'll cut me in half. But that's not to be today, so you can stop your silly hissing. I am not afraid, for now is not the time. Someday I'll test you, and you will win, but you will go also. You kill all you touch, but someday the white men will get you. They also kill all that they touch."

Toby stared at the crocodiles as if mesmerized, and it was a half hour before he finally got up and went back to the airboat. As he walked away he said, "I'll see you again soon, long snouts. When they return, tell your two friends that Toby Tiger was here."

Toby Tiger was a twenty-five-year-old Seminole Indian, five feet ten inches tall, with deeply browned skin, high cheekbones and the almost oriental look of pure Seminoles. His body was hard and muscular, his legs slightly bowed, and his eyes as black as his raven hair.

Toby had been born on a Florida Everglades hammock southwest of the Tamiami Trail, the highway running through the Everglades from Naples to Miami. He had always loved all things about this land, and his boyhood days were filled with hunting and fishing and running free with the wind and sleeping beneath the open-sided chickee huts and exploring the vast River of Grass and the hammocks. By the time he was ten, he knew almost every hammock and mangrove swamp from the Ten Thousand Islands to Whitewater Bay.

Toby's mother and father had insisted that he get as much schooling as possible, and when he reached school age, they forced him to go out to the Tamiami Trail each

morning and catch the yellow bus that transported
Indian children to the white school in Everglades City.
Each day as he rode the bus his mind was filled only
with anticipation of returning that afternoon to the
Glades. He studied the books and the figures by the light
of an open fire each night, but he did so only to please
his mother and father.

In 1965, when Toby was fifteen and in the ninth
grade, a flash fire swept over the hammock, killing his
parents and reducing the chickees to ashes. It was said
that the fire was set by white hunters trying to flush deer
from the sawgrass. Toby escaped death by being in
school that day, and when he returned to the hammock
and found what had happened, his schooling was ended
forever. He buried his mother and father on a remote
hammock in the old Seminole way, in crude cypress
coffins placed on top of the ground and then covered by
a small frame of pond cypress poles.

Toby went to live in the camp of his grandfather and
grandmother north of the Tamiami Trail, and his days
were spent in exploring this new land; but the grief of his
mother and father's deaths always lingered. Although the
bitterness and sadness never really left, he spent many
happy days with his grandparents and came to love them
as he did his parents.

Several years later his grandfather's camp was se-
lected as the site of the new Miami International Airport, and they were told they must move because the
land was to be drained and cleared and filled. The giant
concrete runways were eventually built, but the international airport was never to be. Protests by conservation

groups halted the project but not before a large section of the swamp's heart had been destroyed. The runways were now used as training facilities by several airlines.

Toby's grandfather decided to build his new camp on a hammock southwest of the Trail where destruction would be slower in coming. At the time of the move, the grandmother became ill, and less than a month after the new chickees were completed and the ground cleared, she died. Toby's grandfather lived by the old Seminole ways, and he would not remain in the camp after a death. They buried the grandmother on the hammock with Toby's mother and father, then they burned the chickees and moved once again to a hammock several miles west of the deserted camp.

Toby remained on the hammock with his grandfather for two years, but it became increasingly difficult for them to live off the land. The drainage canals and dikes built by white men turned the water away from the marsh. During periods of draught, which came more and more often, the land dried up, killing the deer and other animals and the fish. Then when great rains did come, and water could not escape the diked areas quickly enough, the flooding drowned the deer and small animals. But Toby's grandfather refused to even discuss going elsewhere, insisting that he had moved enough and would spend his remaining days here regardless.

Toby then left the hammock and took odd jobs wherever he could find them, returning to the camp each weekend with what supplies he could buy. He worked on road repair crews and in service stations and on cattle ranches, living temporarily in the chickees of any Seminole family who would accept him. Most often he would sleep on the ground alone beneath cabbage palms. For a time he wrestled alligators for tourists along the Tamiami Trail and in the Seminole Indian Village on the small reservation at Dania, but none of the jobs he would hold for long. As soon as he had money, he would return to his grandfather's hammock with supplies and remain there until he was forced to seek work again.

While helping with a cattle roundup on the Big Cypress Reservation, he met Lucy Cypress, daughter of Reverend Charlie Cypress, the reservation's Seminole Baptist preacher. He went back as often as possible to visit her, sometimes even missing the weekend with his grandfather, and two years ago they were married by her father in the concrete-block church on the reservation.

Toby then rented for fifty dollars a month an abandoned hunting camp belonging to a man in Miami, and he took Lucy there to make their home. The camp was located on the Loop Road, which was a twenty-four mile stretch of limestone dirt that left the Tamiami Trail at Monroe Station, looped out through the swamp and came back to the Trail at Forty Mile Bend. Most of the Loop Road was uninhabited except for a few hunting cabins and the small village of Pinecrest, which contained only a cafe catering to hunters, a small general store, and the Gator Hook Lodge. But more and more lots along the road were being sold for weekend cabins.

Lucy did not want to live in this remote place so far from her mother and father and the type of reservation life she knew, but she loved Toby deeply and would follow him wherever he chose to go and live however he wished to live.

For the past year Toby had worked with a state highway department crew, chopping bushes, cutting grass and cleaning drainage canals alongside the highway. And each Saturday morning he took supplies to his grandfather's hammock.

When Toby left Allapattah Flats he headed eastward, again driving the airboat at full speed. He slowed only once when he came to a small pond partially covered with water lilies.

Toby cut the engine and picked up a cypress pole in the bottom of the boat, then he pushed the boat slowly into the center of the pond. Suddenly he dove from the boat and disappeared beneath the surface. A startled black bass bolted from a clump of pickerel weeds, sending a turbulent wave rushing across the top of the water.

In a moment Toby came up clutching a large snapping turtle. He threw the turtle into the boat on its back, then he climbed in and said, "You'll make a good stew for Grandfather. I almost missed sight of you, but you didn't hide quick enough."

He did not stop again until he reached a large hammock several miles to the east. From a distance he could see the smoke of a fire drifting above the cabbage palms, and then he made the engine backfire several times. When he reached the shore, the old man was waiting for him.

Toby rammed the boat ashore, jumped out and hugged his grandfather. The old man said, "I am glad to

see you, Toby. I always hear you coming. No one but
Toby Tiger drives the airboat with such thunder." He
spoke in the old Seminole way, pronouncing each word
slowly and distinctly, as if reading from an unseen book.

Toby climbed back into the boat, picked up the
package and said, "I've brought many things this time,
Grandfather. I have corn meal and flour, sugar and salt,
rice, a package of sliced ham, two boxes of shotgun
shells, bread and coffee."

The old man smiled at the sight of the sack. He said,
"Did you bring tobacco?"

"Yes. I have a large tin. And before you ask, I also
brought sugar buns."

"That is good. You are a fine grandson, Toby. I have
thanked my son many times for bringing you to life."

They walked along a path to the center of the hammock where there were two chickees, one for cooking
and one for sleeping. Toby put the package on a plank
shelf in the cooking chickee, then they sat on benches at
a cypress table beneath a cabbage palm. Each time Toby
returned to the hammock it brought floods of memories
of the days he lived here. He said, "How've you been this
week, Grandfather?"

"For one who has lived seventy-eight or more sum-
mers, I seem to manage well enough. But it is getting
harder each day to find food, and I have a great fear now
of fire." The old man was about the same height as Toby,
but his body was as frail as bamboo. His skin was baked
black and deeply wrinkled, and his hair a solid white.
His misty eyes were squinting and tired.

"It is very dry and dangerous everywhere," Toby said.

"I cannot count the days it has been since we had rain, and the water in places is down three feet and more. We need much rain."

"It is not just the rain," the grandfather said. "The white men's canals and dikes have turned the water away from the marsh. Someday all this will be no more. There were times when food out here was plentiful, fish so thick I caught them with my hands, and deer so many that I killed them easily with the bow and arrow anytime I needed meat. Now I cannot find even one deer to kill with the shotgun."

For a moment Toby hesitated to say what he promised Lucy he would ask once again, then he spoke cautiously, "What you say is true, Grandfather. The land out here is dying. This is no longer a fit place for you. Will you not come now and live in my camp, or move to the reservation if you would rather do that? There are many people on the reservation you know from the old days."

Just as Toby expected, the old man's eyes flashed. He said, "I will never do this thing, Toby! I have lived all my years as I live now, and what time I have left will be spent here. I will die here, and then I will lie with your grandmother and your mother and father on the hammock in the marsh."

Toby felt no surprise from the words. He said, "As you wish, Grandfather. But if you ever decide to leave, you must tell me this. I only wish I could live here with you, but this is not to be."

"No, it is not to be. You have a child in your woman now. This would be no place for you or for them. Those days are gone forever, Toby. Soon now it will be no more."

"Are you hungry?" Toby asked, wanting to change the subject and cause no further disturbance to the old man. "I'll fix a nice dinner of ham and rice."

"I already have a stew of rabbit. We will eat together, but I wish that the stew was turtle."

Toby jumped up and said, "I forgot that I brought you a turtle, a large one about thirty pounds. It's in the boat. I'll get it while you dish up the stew."

When Toby returned with the turtle, two steaming bowls were on the table. The old man said, "Just leave him on his back and I will clean him later." When Toby put him down, the turtle's legs kicked frantically, trying to right itself.

After they finished eating, the old man went to the chickee and returned with a wooden box resembling an old army trunk. He placed it on the table, opened it and removed a bundle wrapped tightly in deer hide. He said, "I am old, Toby, and I am becoming very tired. The days are not many. There are things here I want you to have. They have always been for you, but I have waited for the time, and the time is now."

Toby watched curiously as his grandfather untied the package. He placed on the table a multi-colored knee-length dress, a pair of knee-length buckskin moccasins, a buckskin belt with a sheathed knife, a ceremonial sash, and a turban with three egret plumes. Toby stared at the items with wonder.

"These were the warrior clothes of my grandfather," the old man said. "He wore them beside Osceola, and then in battles at the side of Wild Cat and Billy Bowlegs.

He was an honorable warrior, and he was never defeated until the time came when he had to flee with others and hide in the swamps to escape the white soldiers, and he was not defeated then. It was a long war, and it also touched my father. But in the end it was all for nothing. The white soldiers were too many and too strong, and there was no way to stop them. But if my grandfather and father and others had not refused defeat and hidden in the swamps, there would be none of us here now. They did an honorable thing. The warrior clothes were passed down from my grandfather to my father and to me. They are for you now, Toby, and your son after you. Keep them with honor."

Toby did not know what to say. He ran his hands across the cloth which was still firm after so many decades. "Are you sure you want to do this, Grandfather?" he asked.

"They are yours now," the old man repeated. "And there is one thing more." From the bundle he took a small buckskin pouch attached to a thin strap and put it gently onto the table. "This is the sacred medicine bag," he said. "There have never been more than three true ones among our people. When I was but a young man, and we lived on a hammock many days' journey from here, the wind for several days was filled with the pollen of the sawgrass, so thick it was hard to see. We knew this to be a bad omen, a sign of great wind. Many left the hammock and went deep into the swamp, but others did not leave. A great hurricane came out of the south, bringing both wind and water, and much death. All the people who remained on the hammock were killed, and among them was the medicine man. When I went back after the storm, I found this hanging on the limb of a gumbo limbo tree. I have kept it all these years, and now it is yours. It is very sacred, and it has great power. Use it only for good, and never for evil. It will show you the way to the Great Spirit in the sky."

Toby picked up the pouch and turned it over and over in his hands. He said, "If it will do what you say, Grandfather, you need it more than I."

"I need it no more. I have seen the way and I know the way. When you live my years, and you live alone on the marsh as I have lived, you see many things others cannot see. Since the death of your father and mother, your heart has been troubled, my grandson. I know this. I have seen anguish and hatred in your eyes many times. You have not accepted things as they must be. What you wish most is gone forever. The peace you seek must be found only within yourself. Know this, Toby. Use the medicine bag wisely, and it will help you find the way."

Toby wrapped all of the things in the deer hide and tied them tightly, then he rose and said, "I'll keep all these things as you have kept them, Grandfather. They'll be passed to my son with honor. And I thank you more than you can know. But I must go now."

The old man said, "The next time you come, Toby, can you bring pork chops? I have wanted this very much lately."

"I'll bring a whole hog," Toby said, watching his grandfather carefully. "We'll cook it and eat it together."

"We could not eat a whole hog," the old man chuckled. "Pork chops would do fine."

They walked back to the boat together. Toby once
again hugged the old man, then he got into the airboat
and shot away quickly across the marsh.

TWO

≈≈≈≈≈≈≈

Toby's camp was located on a half acre of cleared ground, and the main facility was an old City of Miami bus with the seats removed and the tireless wheels resting four feet off the ground on cypress blocks. Inside the bus there was a small refrigerator, several shelves for canned goods and other staples, a counter with an electric hotplate, a small wall cabinet, a table with four chairs, another small table holding a portable Singer sewing machine, and a sagging double bed. Blue cotton curtains covered the windows facing the road.

Behind the bus Toby had built a chickee from thin cypress poles with a roof of thatched palmetto fronds. An iron gate propped up on concrete blocks was beneath the chickee, and here Lucy did most of the cooking over an open fire because it was usually too hot to cook inside the bus. Also, Toby preferred his food cooked this way. There was a cypress table with two benches beside the chickee.

Water came from a faucet above a well just to the east of the bus, and here Toby had built a small enclosed shower stall which operated from the same faucet. This was done at the insistence of Lucy. At the back of the clearing there was an outdoor privy with a tin roof.

A small section of the clearing was used as a garden where Lucy grew tomatoes, corn, squash, okra, and peppers. Chickens roamed freely, pecking at anything that moved.

It was just past noon when Toby returned from his grandfather's hammock. When he came into the clearing, Lucy was sitting beside the grate, stirring stew in a blackened iron pot. He went into the bus and put the buckskin bundle into a cabinet, then he took a can of beer from the refrigerator and came back to the table.

Lucy looked up and said, "How was your grandfather?"

"I'm not sure if he is well or not. But he wouldn't even talk about coming here to live."

"I wish he'd change his mind," she said.

Lucy, six years younger than Toby, was five feet tall with black hair flowing halfway down her back. Her slim body was beginning to show the child she had carried within her for five months. Her skin was pale and not deeply burned by wind and sun as was Toby's. Her wide black eyes and high cheekbones accentuated a face of unusual beauty. Instead of the traditional long Seminole skirt, she wore a pair of black slacks, an orange blouse and leather sandals.

Toby took a deep drink of beer and said, "Are you feeling well?" He was pleased about the baby and overly concerned for her condition.

"Yes. I'm fine." She put the wooden spoon into the pot and came over to the table. "Are you still going to take me to see my mother and father tomorrow?" she asked.

"Yes. We'll leave as early as you wish."

"Josie Billie came by here this morning," Lucy said. "He wanted to see you, and said he would come again later. Do you wish to eat now?"

"I'm not hungry. I ate with Grandfather before I left the hammock."

"I'm not hungry either," Lucy said. "And I have sewing to do." She got up and went into the bus.

Toby had just started carving an alligator from a block of cypress wood when the 1970 Ford Mustang pulled into the camp and stopped. Josie Billie got out of the car and came over to the table. He was a Seminole the same age and build as Toby, but he wore a thin beard along his lower jaws. He lived in a village along the Trail that was open to tourists. One of the attractions inside the village was alligator wrestling, and Josie was in charge of this part of the tourist trade.

Toby motioned for his visitor to sit down. He said, "Hello, Josie. How are you and the 'gators?"

"Not too good right now," Josie said. "That's why I came to see you."

"You want a beer?" Toby asked.

"Yes. And I've got a fifth of Old Crow in the car. I'll get it too."

Toby went into the bus to get the beer while Josie brought the bottle from the car. They took seats at the table, passed the bottle and then opened the beers.

Josie said, "We've got an old bull 'gator in one of the pits who thinks he wants to mate. It's making him so ornery he's snapping at anything that moves. He almost bit the tail off another bull. We've got to get him out of the pit with the other bulls and into the big pen, but nobody can handle him. Can you come to the village and help?"

"Yes, I can do this," Toby replied. "I have nothing to do this afternoon. But if he does make love when we get him into the pen, don't watch it. My grandfather once told me that if you watch someone make love, either a man or an animal, you'll go blind."

"That doesn't bother me," Josie said. "The only thing I want to see of that old bull is his tail going over the side of the pit. You want to come down and wrestle for the tourists tomorrow? Sunday is usually a good day. You can make yourself a few bucks."

"No," Toby replied. "I'm taking Lucy to the reservation to see her mother and father."

Josie took another drink from the bottle and pushed it toward Toby. He said, "You ought to come to the village and wrestle every day. You could make as much doing that as you make working on the road. You're the best 'gator man in the Glades, and you know it."

"I couldn't stand having those white tourists stare at me that much," Toby said. "I'll do it for you sometimes, but not all of the time."

"You'd get used to the tourists. Most of the time I don't even know they're there. We take their money and that's the end of it."

Toby drank again from the bottle, then he said, "I would never get used to it. Whites are the lowest of all things. They're chicken snakes."

Josie looked at Toby curiously and said, "They're not

so bad as that, Toby. I thought you liked Big Jim Bentley
and several other whites living on the Loop."

"They're different," Toby said. "Sometimes I think
they're part Indian. But I couldn't stand those white
tourists. I'll wrestle for you sometimes, but not all of the
time."

"Anytime you want to make a few extra bucks it's up
to you. Money is money no matter whose pocket it
comes from. And I'll sure appreciate it if you'll help get
that loco 'gator out of the pit."

Toby got up and said, "I'll leave in a few minutes. I
can't go as fast as that Mustang, but I'll be there shortly
after you."

As soon as Josie pulled out of the clearing, Toby went
into the bus and said to Lucy, "I'm going to the Osceola
Village to help Josie with a bad 'gator. I'll be back as soon
as I can."

Lucy stopped the sewing machine. "Are you coming
back by Monroe Station?" she asked.

"Yes. I haven't cashed my check and paid the rent."

"There are things we need," she said. "I've made a
list. Will you get them?"

"I'll stop at Monroe Station on the way back."

Toby went outside and walked to his old 1960 Ford
pickup. The truck had originally been red, but now it
was covered solidly with white limestone dust. He got
into the cab and cranked the engine, sending a huge puff
of smoke out of the exhaust pipe and across the clearing.

THREE

~~~~~~

Toby turned south on the Tamiami Trail and stopped several miles later when he reached a paved road leading off the left side of the highway. A tall cyclone fence guarded the property, but the gate was open. This was the entrance to the airport that had taken the land of his grandfather. A sign beside the gate read: "No trespassing except for official airport business. Gates closed from 7 p.m. to 7 a.m. For information call Miami International Airport Administrative Office in Miami." For a moment Toby stared at the strip of black asphalt leading into the swamp, then he cursed to himself and drove away quickly.

When he reached Forty Mile Bend, the highway turned directly east and ran arrow-straight across the Everglades toward Miami. It was along this section that many Indians lived, and their chickees could be seen in clumps of banana trees along the highway. Several Indians were fishing in the drainage canal paralleling the highway, and others walked aimlessly along the borders of the road. Brightly colored signs offered airboat rides, alligator wrestling, village tours, souvenirs and cold beer.

Toby pulled in when he reached the John Osceola

Indian Village. Facing the highway there was a souvenir store, and a tall board fence surrounded the rest of the village. Inside the store there were racks of handmade Seminole skirts, blouses and jackets. Counters were piled high with Indian dolls and a variety of items carved from cypress. A sign over a rear door inside the shop read: "$1.25 each to enter village. Alligator wrestling 50¢ extra."

It was here that Josie Billie and six other Seminole families lived. Toby greeted John Osceola and his wife as he went through the souvenir store and into the village. Several groups of tourists were walking about, looking into the chickees and snapping pictures. Indian children chased each other around the compound, throwing rocks and ignoring the tourists until offered twenty-five cents to stand before a camera; then they stopped and smiled into the lens, palms outstretched.

The wrestling pits were located behind another fence on the west side of the village. Behind the pits there was a three-acre pen containing more than two hundred alligators.

Toby found Josie Billie standing beside the second of three wrestling pits. Several other Seminole men were also there, but no tourists. They were all looking into the pit. When he saw Toby approaching, Josie turned and said, "He's even worse than before, Toby. We're glad you're here. We can't do a thing with this old fool."

Toby walked to the low concrete wall surrounding the pit. Inside, there were five bull alligators, one with a nasty red gash across its tail. The largest was about sixteen feet long, and he looked to be very old.

Josie said, "There's nothing worse than a bull 'gator in heat, and this idiot is too old to even have it on his mind. I don't know what's the matter with him. He acts plumb loco, and he's been this way for several days."

"Maybe he just wants out of that pit for a while," Toby said, studying the alligator carefully. "If he does, I would sure know how he feels."

"Maybe so, but he won't let anybody give him any help in getting out."

Toby took off his shirt, kicked off his old brogan shoes, and removed a leather thong holding a large crocodile tooth that he always wore around his neck. Then he picked up a stick and jumped into the pit, approaching the old bull from the rear. When he touched him on the back with the stick, the 'gator wheeled around quickly and snapped the stick in half, then he opened his jaws and hissed menacingly, snapping again at Toby. Toby stepped back and said, "He may be old, but he's still filled with fire. Do you have rope ready?"

"We have rope," Josie replied. "We're ready when you are."

Toby walked slowly around the alligator several times, and each time the 'gator turned to face him. The other alligators in the pit paid no heed to what was happening. Toby finally turned to Josie and said, "He's following me, and I have to get behind him. Come in here and get his attention."

Josie climbed into the pit and waved a stick at the alligator, and Toby eased away slowly. The 'gator sprang at Josie, snapping at the stick and hissing. The moment the 'gator's attention was turned away from him, Toby sprang catlike onto its back, locking his arms and legs around the bull's huge body.

For a split second the alligator lay still, then the pit exploded in violence. The 'gator twisted over and over, jumping and bucking and then tumbling again and again. Toby felt his body being rammed into the ground. The 'gator's hide cut into his flesh, sending sharp pains through his chest, but he locked his arms and legs around the body tighter and tighter and held on desperately. The other alligators scrambled out of the way as Toby and the old bull thrashed around and around the pit. Several times the breath was knocked from Toby, and his mouth was clogged with dirt.

Finally the violence slowed. Toby pulled himself forward and snapped the 'gator's jaws shut, then he flipped him on his back. Josie and four other men pounced on the 'gator immediately, tying his jaws with rope. Toby was still holding on as Josie shouted, "Let go, Toby! It's done!"

Toby pushed himself to his feet. He stared at the old bull, now lying motionless, then he walked over to the wall. Blood was oozing from several cuts on his chest, and he was covered with dirt. He spat dirt from his mouth and said, "Damn! That was a rough ride. The old devil was almost more than I could handle."

The other men picked up the bull and dragged him over the wall and into the large pen. Josie looked after them and said, "I hope the old fool soon works off his mad. I could never have stayed on him like that. We should have let the tourists in here and charged five bucks a head to watch. You can clean up at my chickee, and you probably need a drink after that ride."

Toby picked up the leather thong with the crocodile tooth and put it back around his neck. He gathered up his shirt and shoes, and then he followed Josie back into the village where he bathed himself at a hydrant, letting the cool water gush over his head. Josie took a carton of beer from an ice box, then they went outside the rear of the village fence and sat on the bank of the drainage canal.

For several minutes they drank in silence, and then Toby said, "Someday I'll try that with a crocodile."

Josie said, "You do, and that will be the end of you. There would be nothing left but cracked bones and your flesh in the croc's belly. You wouldn't stand a chance."

"You're probably right," Toby said, "but I'd try. And I'd rather end my days in the belly of a croc than be dead on the ground and eaten by vultures."

Josie looked at Toby curiously and said, "Toby, sometimes you're as strange as the old 'gator we took out of the pit." He finished his beer and opened another. "But you ought to come here and wrestle all the time. You could make good money. Nobody can handle a 'gator like you can."

Toby spoke absently, the words directed not to Josie or to anyone, "I'll wrestle for you some of the time, but not all of the time. I couldn't stand the white tourists."

Toby stopped the truck when he reached the store at Monroe Station. The two-story wooden structure, housing a combination grocery and cafe, was plastered with dozens of garish signs designed to attract the attention of tourists. One large sign in front offered wild hog ham and eggs for breakfast, and a wild hog bar-b-que dinner. The second story served as living quarters for the owners, Big Jim and Suzie Bentley. There were also gas pumps and a small garage adjoining the main building, and this was the only facility for ten miles in either direction. Across the highway there was a grouping of ten chickees where several Seminole families lived.

Toby parked beside the building and went inside. Several people were sitting at tables eating, and two men were at the cafe counter drinking beer. The inside of the building was just as cluttered as the outside. Deer antlers and photos of hunting kills and fish strings covered the walls. When he went into the grocery section, Toby found Big Jim Bentley sitting on the counter, munching a piece of cheese and drinking beer from a paper milkshake cup. Bentley was a tall man with a tough, muscular body and penetrating brown eyes. He was in his middle forties, but a short-cropped brown beard made it difficult to judge his true age.

Bentley flicked his hand in greeting and said, "Hi, Toby. What can I do for you?"

"I need to cash my check and get supplies. I have a list that Lucy sent. And I also want two cartons of beer."

Bentley took the slip of paper and studied the list of supplies. He said, "You know you're behind with the rent, don't you? You want me to take it out of the check first?" He acted as a broker and collected rent from several people along the Loop Road, sending the money on to the owners after deducting a small fee. He also collected electric bills for the power company serving the Loop.

After deductions, Toby's weekly check from the road department was just under sixty dollars, and from this he also had to supply his grandfather. He said, "There won't be enough, Mr. Bentley. Besides the supplies, I need gas for the truck and the airboat. Take out half the rent, and I'll pay the rest Monday afternoon. I gigged frogs last night, and I'll gig again tonight and tomorrow night. Then I'll sell the legs to the restaurant in Ochopee on my way to work Monday and give you the money that afternoon."

Bentley seemed unconcerned. Toby was often late with the rent but he always paid. "That suits me, Toby. While I'm filling the list, go in there and tell Suzie to give you a cold beer on the house."

"That would be good," Toby smiled. "It's been a long hot day, and I wrestled a real bad alligator this afternoon."

"Don't see how you can do anything like that in this heat. I don't think I've ever seen it so hot for June. I could fry eggs on the highway. This morning I was out in the swamp and saw smoke coming off a wild hog's back. If we don't get rain soon, this whole damned place is going to explode. I'd rather stay under the air conditioner and drink beer."

Toby sat at the counter while Bentley gathered the supplies. Those in the cafe who were tourists watched Toby with interest. This was the closest they had come to a Seminole, and they relished the opportunity to stare.

Bentley helped Toby take the bags outside and load them into the truck. Before he left, Toby filled the truck

and two ten-gallon cans with gasoline, then he turned to
Bentley and said, "Thanks, Mr. Bentley. I'll bring the rest
of the rent Monday afternoon."

"Don't worry about it," Bentley replied. "And you
might save a couple of frog legs for me."

"I'll bring a dozen for your dinner," Toby said, "and
there'll be no charge."

As soon as Toby turned down the Loop Road, the
truck churned up a billowing cloud of white limestone
dust. Trees and bushes beside the road were solid white
with dust and looked as if they were covered with snow.
The constant holes in the road caused the old pickup to
bang, rattle and buck as if it would fall apart at any
moment.

Both sides of the road led into an almost impenetrable swamp of pond cypress and wax-myrtle and
palmetto. There had been no rain for more than four
months, and the entire area was a tinderbox. Several
small bridges that once carried traffic over flowing
streams now led over powder-dry, cracked earth.

Toby's place was about halfway along the Loop
Road, and the stretch of road just to the north of his
camp narrowed to little more than one lane. Limbs of
trees formed a solid canopy over the road, creating a
dimly lit tunnel. Dust drifting from the limbs made it
look as if ice were dripping from the trees.

When Toby pulled from the road, the boiling dust
cloud followed him, bathing everything in his camp with
an additional layer of white. He parked the truck behind
the bus and took the packages inside, then he opened a
beer and came out to the table beside the chickee.

Lucy was sitting on the ground beneath the chickee. She said to him, "Did you get all of the things?"

"Yes. But I didn't have enough left to pay all the rent. I'll gig frogs again tonight and tomorrow night and sell the legs on my way to work Monday, then I'll pay the rest of the rent."

"I wish you wouldn't go into the swamp so much at night. It's dangerous, and one of these nights a bugger will get you."

"I'm not afraid of buggers," Toby said. "I'm a bugger myself. And we need the extra money. Everything costs so much now, and I never seem to have enough."

Lucy got up and came over to the table. "You're drinking too much, Toby," she said without emotion or threat.

For a moment Toby made no response. He looked across the darkening clearing and into the woods, as if something had suddenly caught his attention. Then he said, "Yes, I know." For the past year his drinking had become steady but had caused no harm to himself or others. The only time he didn't drink or wish to drink was when he was alone in the swamp or in the Glades with his grandfather.

Lucy said nothing more of this. "Do you wish to eat now?" she asked.

"I'm very hungry. It was a bad afternoon with Josie."

She went to the grill and dished up two plates of chicken stew, then she brought over a Dutch oven of hot biscuits. Toby took the plate and ate eagerly.

As soon as the meal was done and the dishes cleaned, Lucy went into the bus and started running the sewing machine. Toby walked to the back of the chickee and returned with a gig mounted on a long cane pole. He called to the bus, "I'm going now. I'll return soon."

Lucy looked out the door and said, "Be careful, Toby."

Toby picked up one of the gasoline cans and walked across the clearing and into the darkness of the swamp. Far in the distance, somewhere close by the bank of Lost Creek, the shrill cry of a panther broke the stillness of the night.

FOUR

Dawn had not come the next morning when Toby and Lucy climbed into the pickup truck for the trip to the Big Cypress Reservation. Lucy wanted to start early so she could spend as much time as possible with her parents. They did not go to the reservation often, and she had been homesick lately, although she would never mention this to Toby.

Toby did not share Lucy's enthusiasm for the trips to the reservation. He liked and respected her parents, but he had never accepted the Christian faith, looking upon it as the white man's religion. His parents and grandparents had lived by the old Seminole traditions, believing in a supreme being but not accepting the Christian preachings as the only true faith. Lucy's father knew of Toby's reluctance to accept Christian faith, and he wished to convert him if possible. But Toby resisted his efforts.

Toby followed the Trail until it met Highway 29, then he turned north toward Immokalee. The sky was streaked with red as he passed Copeland, and soon they reached the junction of Alligator Alley, the toll road running from Naples to Fort Lauderdale, cutting a wide swath through the heart of the Big Cypress Swamp. At this hour on a Sunday morning the highway was empty, and Toby pulled through the usually dangerous but now deserted intersection and continued north.

From Immokalee he headed east on a narrow paved road running through vast areas of cattle country. The open prairie was broken occasionally by clumps of cabbage palms and pines, and cow egrets swarmed after herds of grazing cattle, eating whatever insects the cattle exposed.

The entrance to the reservation was marked by a sign warning visitors against hunting or fishing on reservation land. Soon they came to the residential section where some of the Indian families had built concrete-block houses, some lived in house trailers, and others still lived in the open-sided chickees. There were also two small trading posts and the Baptist Church.

Lucy's parents lived in a concrete-block house beside the small church. In another section of the churchyard there was a large chickee where families gathered to spread dinner after services, and for other social occasions. Most of the Seminoles who had built concrete houses had also built a chickee in the yard.

When Toby arrived at the house, he remained in the truck and said to Lucy, "I'm going to visit some friends for a while. I'll be back later."

Lucy said, "The services begin at ten. Pappa will be disappointed if you're not there."

"I know," Toby said. "I'll be back in time for the services."

As he watched Lucy go into the house, Toby regretted his decision not to go in with her. He hesitated for a moment, thinking of getting out and following her, then he pulled from the yard and moved along the paved road.

Toby drove slowly, looking at the block houses and the clusters of chickees. He turned when he came to a road leading to the maintenance barn for the cattle trucks and farm equipment. The place was deserted, so he drove back to one of the stores, and it was also closed. Then he drove a half-mile east and parked beside a narrow dirt trail leading through a thick grove of oaks.

The ground beneath the trees was thickly covered with leaves, and he made no sound as he approached the cluster of chickees. A dog suddenly ran into the path and snarled. A voice called from the camp, and the dog retreated.

This was the camp of Miami Billie, the tribal medicine man. Toby had met him once during a cattle roundup but did not really know him. When he entered the camp, Miami Billie was sitting at a table beneath one of the chickees. Nearby, an old woman, dressed in an ankle length dress with pounds of glass beads around her neck, was cooking on an open grill.

Toby sat across from the man and said, "I'm Toby Tiger, grandson of Keith Tiger who lives in the marsh west of the Trail. I'm married to Lucy Cypress, daughter of Charlie Cypress, the Baptist preacher."

Miami Billie was in his late sixties but looked much older. His hair was white, and his face deeply lined. He looked across at Toby and said, "How is your grandfather?"

"He seems to be fine. I've heard him speak of you."
Toby thought for a moment of telling Miami Billie about
the ancient medicine bag his grandfather had given him,
but he decided against this for fear that the old man
might want it.

For a moment there was no further conversation, and
then the medicine man said, "Do you want a love potion?
I can make you one for two dollars."

Toby laughed. "No. I have no need of that. My wife
is five months with child."

Miami Billie's stern expression did not change. He
said, "Have you had dreams lately?"

"No. I have had no dreams."

"Then what is your problem?"

"I have no problem," Toby said, beginning to feel
uneasy. "This is just a visit."

"Oh," the medicine man said, immediately losing
interest in his visitor.

Toby got up and said, "It's been good to see you,
Miami Billie. I'll tell grandfather when I see him again."

"Come back if you have dreams. If you have dreams,
I can make a cure for you."

Toby walked back through the grove and then drove
east again. When he came to a large drainage canal he
parked, sat on the bank and threw rocks into the water.
He knew that the services would begin soon and that he
should return to the church, but he continued to sit on
the bank for another hour.

People were beneath the giant chickee, spreading
food on long tables, when Toby returned to the house.
He joined Lucy and her parents at one of the tables.

After eating, they all went to the house and sat in cane
rockers on the front porch.

Lucy's father was a tall man with a lean, wiry body.
During the week he helped with the cattle operation,
and his face was burned deep brown by sun and wind.

For several minutes they all rocked in silence, and
then Lucy's father said, "We missed you at the services,
Toby."

This was the conversation Toby had tried to avoid.
He said, "I was visiting friends and lost track of the time.
I'm sorry."

Lucy's father continued to rock. He said, "Lucy tells
me you're still working on the road, and also that it's very
dry now on the Loop. If you want to come and live on
the reservation for a while, you're always welcome.
There's less danger here of fire."

Toby wanted to get up and walk away but knew that
he must not do this. He feared the effect of his words as
he said, "What would I do if I came here, become a
white man? Take up the white ways and live in a concrete
house? They're making white men out of all of you who
live on the reservation. I'll never do this so long as the
marsh is still there."

Lucy glanced at Toby nervously but remained silent.
Her father said, "You have much bitterness in your heart,
Toby. Do you still blame the white people for the death
of your parents? That was a bad thing, but it was many
years ago and is best forgotten now."

"I'll never forget. They were the cause of it, and
they're not friends of the Indian."

"That's not true," the reverend said, his voice still

calm. "The white man has done many good things for our people. They're now building schools and medical clinics and other things. And did they not give us this land?"

"They gave us this land?" Toby questioned. "They gave us nothing! Once we owned all the land, and they took it from us. Then they gave us back this small part, and now they're taking this back too, bit by bit. First it was canals and dikes, and then a highway, and then another highway, and then power lines. Soon there will be nothing left but what is useless to them. They destroy all that they touch."

Lucy's father was becoming as uncomfortable as Toby, but he knew he must pursue the conversation as best he could and try to change Toby's attitude. He said, "Toby, the Christian way is to forgive. That is what most of our people have done. If you do not have it in your heart to do this, then you don't understand the ways of God."

Toby calmed his voice and said, "I know that God is everything. God is the land and the water and the trees and the animals, and they are destroying Him. God will soon be dead."

"Do not believe such a thing, Toby!" the reverend admonished. "That's not true. God will never be dead, and if you believe what you say, then you've never seen the true face of God as I have."

Toby stopped rocking. Sweat formed on his forehead, and he wished the conversation had never started. He said slowly, "I've seen the face of God, the true face. It was in the swamp during a dry spell. I came to a pond with no water. Fish were flouncing about in the mud, dying. A huge cotton-mouth came over the bank and into the pond. His body was as big as my leg. I said to myself, 'Now the snake will feast on the fish.' He took a fish in his mouth, but he did not eat it. Instead, he carried it over the bank and to a nearby pond with water, and then he turned it loose. He came back and did this again and again. I had never seen such a thing before, and I knew this must be the face of God. While I watched, a white man came up behind me. He too watched the snake take the fish to the other pond and set them free. Then he aimed his rifle and shot the snake through the head. He went into the pond, picked up the remaining fish, put them into a sack and walked away. I couldn't believe what I'd seen. He killed God for a few fish."

Lucy's father didn't make an immediate response. He rubbed the side of his head and looked deeply worried. He finally said, "Toby, you're the husband of my daughter, and you'll soon be the father of my grandchild. We all love you. We're concerned for your life and the life that comes after. If you ever have need of me, I am here."

Toby felt relief that the conversation was ended. He said, "I thank you for your concern, and I haven't meant to offend you. I've only spoken what I feel." Then he got up and said to Lucy, "It is time for us to go now."

Lucy kissed her mother and father and then followed Toby to the truck. They both remained silent during the drive back to Immokalee. Toby was anguished, wishing that he had attended the services whether he wanted to or not, and then enjoyed a pleasant visit with Lucy's parents. He could find no excuse for his behavior regardless of how he felt inside, and worst of all, he also knew that Lucy had been shamed in front of her parents.

Finally he reached over and touched her hand. "I'm sorry, Lucy," he said. "I didn't mean to ruin your visit. I don't know what's wrong with me. I mean only love for your parents."

Tears welled in her eyes as she said, "Pappa was only trying to help. He's a good man, and he meant you no harm."

"I know. And I'm sorry. I'll tell him this the next time we visit, and I'll also listen to him and not argue."

No further words were spoken during the remainder of the trip. When they reached the camp, Lucy prepared a supper of fried chicken and boiled corn she brought back from the reservation, but Toby only picked at the food. For a while he sat at the table beside the chickee and carved on a block of cypress, then he took the gig from the chickee and vanished into the swamp.

FIVE

~~~~~~

I t was the middle of the next week before
Lucy's coolness toward Toby subsided. Toby
worked those few days with no thought of
what he was doing. His mind was dominated by the way
he acted at the reservation, and several times the road
foreman admonished him for careless work. He knew
that what he had done was useless and foolish, and he
was determined to never again become argumentative
with Lucy's father about religion. He would simply listen
and let that be the end of it. Although he regretted what
he had done, he still believed there was only truth in
what he said.

Toby had not yet shown Lucy the things his grandfather had given him. He had placed the buckskin
bundle in the cabinet and covered it with a blanket. It
was now late in the afternoon after supper, and Lucy was
at the outdoor faucet, washing dishes in a tin tub.

Toby went inside and took the bundle from the
cabinet. He untied it carefully and placed each item on
the bed, then he slipped off his faded jeans and put on
the knee-length dress. It fit perfectly. The knee-length
moccasins were also a perfect fit. He strapped on the
belt with the knife, put the ceremonial sash over his

shoulder, and put on the turban with the plumes. All of it seemed as if it had been made for him. Then he put the medicine bag strap around his neck and looked at himself in a mirror on one wall of the bus.

Just then Lucy came inside. She was startled by his appearance, and she said quizzically, "What is that you've got on, Toby? Where did you get such things?"

"Grandfather gave them to me," he said, puffing out his chest. "This is the warrior dress of Grandfather's grandfather. He wore these things when he fought with Osceola and Wild Cat and Billy Bowlegs. They were passed down to his son and then to Grandfather, and now he has given them to me."

"I haven't seen such things before except in picture books," Lucy said. "They're very old and must have great value. It's a wonder they didn't rot."

"They were wrapped tightly in buckskin," Toby said, strutting around the bus, "and they seem to be as good as new. Do you know what this is around my neck?"

Lucy looked at the pouch. "No. I've seen nothing like it before."

"It's the ancient medicine bag," Toby said, fingering the pouch. "Grandfather said there have been only three true ones among our people. He also said it will show the way to the Great Spirit in the sky."

"I don't believe that," Lucy said tartly. "The Christian church is the way. But your grandfather was no medicine man. How did he come to have this thing?"

"When he was very young, he found it in a hammock after all the people had been killed by a hurricane, and he has kept it ever since. He says it is a sacred thing, and

I have always heard that the true medicine bag has great power. Grandfather cautioned me to never use it for evil."

"I don't know how you could use it for anything," Lucy said. "There's no telling what's inside that thing. It's probably filled with crushed bones and frog's tongues and feathers and eyeballs and alligator teeth and no telling what else."

"I'll treat it as a sacred thing," Toby said, disregarding her comment. "Grandfather has lived many years, and he knows the power of the old ways. There are few left so wise as he."

Lucy sat at the sewing machine and inserted a spool of red thread. "Leave the dress out and I'll wash it for you," she said. "It smells musty. I'll be very careful with it."

"I must show these things to Josie Billie," Toby said, again looking into the mirror. "I know he would like to see them."

"If you ever wear them away from the camp, someone will throw a net over you."

"Why?" Toby asked, turning to Lucy. "They're fine things, and they were worn by an honorable man. I'm not ashamed of them."

"It's not a matter of shame. Those things are from the past, and the past is gone forever. They aren't worn anymore. But they are very old and valuable, and I'll be careful when I wash the dress."

Toby took off the things and rewrapped all but the dress, then he put on his jeans.

Lucy said, "Do you plan to gig frogs tonight?"

"Yes. We need the extra money, and the gigging

hasn't been good lately. Most of the ponds are almost dry, and I have seen more snakes than frogs."

Lucy stopped the machine. "I forgot to tell you this morning, but we're out of milk. I should drink milk every day now for the baby. And I also need a spool of blue thread. Can you get these things before you go?"

"Yes. There's plenty of time before the frogs come out. I'll get them at the Hughes Store."

The small store in Pinecrest was closer to Toby's camp than the one on the highway at Monroe Station. He usually traded with Bentley because he could stop there on the way home from work, but he often picked up needed items at Hughes.

The sun dropped from sight into the cypress trees as Toby drove slowly along the pocked road. The lights of the pickup bounced from dust into overhanging limbs and back into dust each time the truck banged loudly into a hole or crossed sections of rutted rock. A family of raccoons ambled slowly across the road and then disappeared quickly in order to escape the choking cloud of white dust following the truck.

After he reached the store and purchased the things for Lucy, he stopped at Don's Bar-B-Que, a rustic wooden building located on a stretch of road halfway between Pinecrest and Toby's camp. It was owned by a man in his early forties, Don Lowry. His cabin was directly across the road from the bar-b-que place, and he also operated a small sawmill where he cut cypress planks and poles which he sold in Naples.

Most of the cafe business was on weekends when the swamp was invaded by hunters and campers from

Miami and Fort Lauderdale and Naples. Now there was a lone station wagon parked in front of the building.

The inside of the cafe contained a long, narrow room with exposed cypress rafters. There were two rows of plank tables and benches, and in one end there was a pool table. The other end was crossed with a cypress counter for serving food and beer. The walls were covered with deer antlers and the stuffed heads of bear and wild hogs.

Don Lowry was behind the counter when Toby entered, and three men were sitting at one of the tables, drinking beer. Toby walked to the counter and said, "Hello, Mr. Lowry. How've you been lately?"

"Dry," Lowry answered. "Don't see you down this way much at night, Toby. You still working on the road?"

"Yes. I had to get some things for Lucy at Hughes."

"Doing any gigging?" Lowry asked.

"Almost every night, but it hasn't been good lately."

"Jim Steelman told me today he isn't having much luck either. He goes every night too. Fact is, that's all he does anymore, sell frogs. We need some real rain to bring the water back up. Ain't no way frogs can live on dry land. You want something, Toby?"

"A six-pack of Bud."

Lowry took a carton of beer from the cooler and handed it to Toby. Toby opened one and put the others in a paper sack, then he paid Lowry and took a seat at one of the tables.

The three men had been watching Toby. They were all dressed in gray khaki pants and shirts, high-topped leather boots, and each wore a long hunting knife at his side.

Toby glanced at the men as he drank the beer. He had never seen any of them before, but this was not unusual. There had been an increasing flow of strangers along the Loop during the past few years.

The men continued to watch Toby closely, then one of them said loudly, "Seems like a stink's come up in here, don't it?"

"Yeah," another replied. "Smells downright bad. Got to where you can't go nowhere anymore and drink a beer without running into a nigger or an Indian. But Indians is the worst of all. You take a Indian, put him in a nice house with a nice yard, and first thing you know the whole place is covered with chicken shit, including his feet. I've seen it happen in Fort Lauderdale. They pure stink, and that's the truth of it."

Toby felt his grip tightening on the beer can, and Lowry got up from a chair and came around the counter.

One of the men said, "I hear tell you try to make one of them Indian broads, she'll fill herself with dirt to keep you from it. Don't know who'd want one of them noway, the way they stink. I couldn't get that close."

Toby suddenly slammed his fist onto the table and said, "Go to hell, you chicken snakes!"

One of the men said, "Well, looka here, fellows. We got us a real live Injun. You going to scalp us, chief? You got a tommy hawk hid in your britches?"

Lowry came over to the table and said, "That's enough, dammit! He hasn't bothered you. You think you can come in here and shoot that kind of crap for the price of a beer? Now get the hell out! And I don't want to see you back again! You understand me?"

The three men got up. One said, "Don't see why you're so worked up, fellow. We didn't do nothing but carry on a private conversation. But we'll tell all our friends who come out here to stay away from your joint. It pure stinks."

"You do that!" Lowry snapped, his face flushed with anger.

Toby was still clutching the beer can with trembling hands as he watched the men go out the door, then he listened as they started the station wagon and drove off toward Monroe Station.

Lowry went back behind the counter and opened a beer for himself, then he came over and sat at the table with Toby. He said, "I'm sorry about that, Toby. Every once in a while I get bastards like that in here. Most folks mind their own business, but there's some who just look for trouble."

"It doesn't matter," Toby said. "There's no harm done. I thought it would end worse than it did." He finished the beer and got up. "I have to go now. Lucy needs the thread."

There was a fraternalistic bond between the few people who lived permanently along the Loop. As Toby went outside, Lowry said with concern, "You take care, Toby."

The anger had finally drained away when Toby rounded a curve and his headlights revealed the station wagon parked along the edge of the road. He approached slowly, and just before he was to pass, the vehicle pulled sideways, blocking his way. The three men got out and walked into the dim glare of the headlights. One turned a flashlight into the pickup cab. "It's him," he said.

The other two men came to the side of the pickup, and one said, "We was hopin' you'd come this way."

"What is it you want?" Toby asked. "I've done nothing to you."

"We don't want anything to cause you to fret. All we want is just to visit a spell. Now why don't you come on out of there and let's talk things over peaceful like?"

"I don't wish trouble with you," Toby said. "Please move your car and let me pass."

"Are you comin' out, or are we comin' in — chicken snake?"

Toby said, "If that's the only way, I'll come out." He stepped out of the truck. "Now what is it you want of me?"

One of the men moved closer and said, "I can handle this by myself, fellows. You just watch and enjoy it." He moved quickly and struck Toby in the face.

The blow caused Toby's ears to ring. He shook his head for a moment, then he pounced on the man as he would an alligator, locking his arms and legs around the man's body. Both of them fell hard into the dust.

As Toby tightened his grip, the man screamed frantically. "Get him off of me! Get him off of me! He's breaking my ribs! Get him off!"

Toby felt the boot smash into his face, then a rain of blows poured onto his head, back and sides. He exerted all of his strength in one final crushing grip, and he could feel bones crack. He heard the man scream once more in agony, and then he heard no more.

When Toby finally became conscious, he pushed himself to a sitting position. Warm blood trickled from the side of his mouth. He sat still for several minutes, wondering how long he had been on the ground.

He got up slowly, walked to the truck and found that the headlights were still on and the motor running. Then he eased himself behind the steering wheel and felt the crunch of broken glass. The windshield was smashed. He swept glass from the seat with his hand, and then he moved the truck forward.

When he came into the bus, Lucy jumped to her feet and gasped, "What has happened to you, Toby?" His body was white with dust, and streaks of red blood creased his face.

He put the package on the table. "Here's the things you wanted," he said. "I'm sorry it took so long."

"For God's sake, Toby, tell me what has happened!"

He leaned against the counter. "I met some white Christian brothers," he said bitterly, "and they didn't like the way I smell."

She could tell he was in pain. She asked anxiously, "Are you hurt badly?"

"No. It is nothing. I'll be fine."

"Do you know who did this to you?"

"I'd never seen any of them before."

Lucy took a cloth and dabbed at his face. She said, "Go and wash yourself, and then I'll treat the cuts."

He pushed her hand away. "I'll do this later, after I have gigged frogs. We need even more extra money now. They smashed my windshield, and I will have to replace it."

She put her hands on his shoulders. "Toby, please don't go off like this," she pleaded. "Go and wash yourself and let me treat the cuts. The frogs don't matter."

"Maybe my smell will drive away the snakes," he said. "The white men said that I stink. I have the smell of chicken shit."

"Toby, please . . ."

Before she could finish, he turned and went outside, then he took the gig from the chickee and disappeared across the clearing and into the swamp.

Lucy put the milk in the refrigerator and returned to the sewing machine. For several minutes she stared at the spool of blue thread, then she dropped her head into her hands and cried softly.

SIX

Toby stopped by Monroe Station the next afternoon after work. Big Jim Bentley was outside in the garage shed, working on a swamp buggy engine. For a moment he didn't notice Toby standing there, and then he looked up and said, "What happened to you, Toby? You look like a bulldozer ran over you."

Both Toby's eyes were blackened and his nose and lips badly swollen. "It's nothing. Just an accident at my camp last night. I tripped and fell into a bench."

Bentley put down the tools and looked at Toby quizzically. "Lots of accidents down your way last night. 'Bout nine o'clock three men from Fort Lauderdale came in here asking about the nearest doctor. One of 'em was in bad shape. Ribs was busted. He was carrying on something awful, muttering something about 'stinkin' Injuns.' They said he tripped and fell across a stump. Must of been a bad night on the Loop with all them accidents. You need something?"

"I need a windshield for my truck."

Bentley looked over at the pickup. "How'd you do that?" he asked. "You trip and fall through it?"

"It was a loose rock on the road."

51

"Must of been some rock to wipe out a whole wind-shield. You want a new one or a used?"

"I don't know. How much would each cost?"

Bentley scratched his head. "Well, I'd say about forty or fifty bucks used, if I can find one. That truck's a pretty old model, and it might be hard to find. A new one would cost somewhere around a hundred and fifty."

"A used one," Toby said quickly. "The truck wouldn't bring a hundred fifty. When would you know if you can find one?"

"I'm going to Naples and to Fort Myers Saturday morning. I'll check all the places there. If I don't find one, I'll try the next time I'm in Miami. If I find one, you want me to put it in?"

"No. I could do this myself."

"In that case, it would cost you only what I have to pay for it. Those things can be a pain to install. I'll get the cheapest one I can find, and I sure better get it pretty quick if I can. You get behind a car on the Loop with this dust the way it is, it'll run you right out of the cab without a windshield."

"It already has," Toby said. "I got behind a car this morning and had to park for more than fifteen minutes to let the dust settle. It almost made me late for work." He stopped and hesitated for a moment, and then he said, "Do you have red paint and a brush in the store?"

"Sure. We stock paint. Won't do you much good to paint anything, though, with the dust so bad."

"I need to paint some things for Lucy inside the bus."

"Just go in the store and tell Suzie what you want."

As Toby started off, Bentley called after him, "Toby!

If you have any more trouble with accidents down your way, you let me know. I've got a whole box full of crowbars and tire tools, and I know how to use them. You hear?"

Toby wished that Bentley didn't suspect the truth. He frowned. "Yes, Mr. Bentley. I'll let you know. But it was only an accident."

After supper that afternoon, Toby took the buckskin bundle from the cabinet. He said to Lucy, "I'm going to the Osceola Village and show these things to Josie. I'll be back in time to gig frogs. Do you need anything from the store?"

"No, I need nothing. But I think you should stay here and rest. You shouldn't have even gone to work today with your face so bad."

"I'm fine, and it doesn't bother me. I'll not be gone long."

On the way to the village, Toby made a mental note of signs along the highway. Although he had traveled the Trail hundreds of times, he had never paid much attention to road signs.

When he reached the village he went through the souvenir store and to the chickee, where he found Josie sitting at a table, finishing a plate of fried fish and corn pone. Josie motioned to Toby to sit down.

"You hungry?" Josie asked. "If you want some fish, we have plenty."

Toby sat on the bench and said, "No thanks. I've already eaten."

Josie plopped a piece of pone into his mouth. "What

happened to you?" he asked curiously, staring at Toby's battered face. "You look like somebody really put one on you."

"It is nothing," Toby replied. "It was only an accident at the camp."

"Last time I saw somebody looking like you, it was after an accident in the Big Coon Bar in Everglades City. It took six deputy sheriffs to break up the accident. I've never seen a 'gator do you up like that. Must of been some accident."

"It is nothing," Toby repeated, not wishing to discuss it further. "I brought something to show you." He opened the bundle and laid the things out on the table.

"What's all this?" Josie exclaimed, running his hand across the dress.

Toby was pleased by Josie's reaction. He said, "These are the warrior clothes of my grandfather's grandfather. He wore them with Osceola and Wild Cat and Billy Bowlegs. Grandfather has given them to me."

"Have you tried them on?" Josie asked, examining the turban.

"Yes. And they fit perfect. It's as if they were made for me. And the cloth is still as good as new."

"There's probably no other like this. You could get a big price for these things in the souvenir store."

"They'll never be for sale," Toby said quickly. "They've been passed down to me, and I'll pass them on to my son."

Josie picked up the pouch. "What's this thing?" he asked.

"It is the ancient medicine bag," Toby replied, "and

it's sacred. Grandfather found it many decades ago when the medicine man was killed by a hurricane. There's no way of knowing how old it is. The bags were passed down from medicine man to medicine man in the old days, and Grandfather says there were never more than three true ones among our people. It's supposed to have great power, and it will show the way to the Great Spirit in the sky."

"Well, you can keep this thing," Josie said, putting the pouch back on the table. "I would probably say the wrong words, or do the wrong dance, and it would explode in my face — or send me down below instead of into the sky. But I have heard from the old people that these things do have magic."

"I will treat it as Grandfather says, as a sacred thing, then maybe I'll find its power."

Josie got up, went to a shelf in the chickee and returned with a bottle of Old Crow. He said, "Let's go sit by the canal and have a drink. I'm dog tired after being in the pits all day. Some days I wish the alligators would win."

Toby followed Josie across the village and out the back gate. Josie took a drink, handed the bottle to Toby and said, "What brings you down here at night? Did you come just to show me the warrior clothes?"

"No, not just that," Toby replied. "There's a thing I'm going to do tonight, and I thought you might want to come along with me."

"Gig frogs?"

"No."

"Then what is it you plan to do?"

"I'm going to paint something on the road signs."

"What?" Josie asked, wondering why Toby was hesitating to say what he meant. "I don't understand what you're trying to say."

Toby said casually, "I am going to paint 'allapattah' on all the signs."

"You've got to be kidding," Josie said, giving Toby a penetrating look. "Have you had too much to drink already? That's just an old word for the long snout crocodile, or maybe even the 'gator. I'm not sure, for I haven't kept up with the old language. But why would you paint this word on a sign? It makes no sense to me."

"The word doesn't really mean crocodile," Toby said. "What it really means is death. The end of all things."

Josie shook his head, disbelieving the whole conversation. Then he realized Toby was serious. He said, "Even if what you say is true, what would be the point? No one but another Seminole would recognize the word as anything. You had as soon write 'yeehaw' as 'allapattah,' for no one would know the difference between 'wolf' and 'crocodile.' The whole thing is silly."

"They will know the difference someday," Toby insisted. "Do you want to come with me or not?"

Josie took another drink from the bottle. After a moment's silence he said, "Toby, I've had accidents too. When I was young, and my mother and father made me go to the white school in Miami, there was a white boy who stopped me outside the building every morning. He would throw up his hand and say, 'How', and then he'd do a war whoop and dance around me in a circle. He did this to me every day, and all the other white boys and girls would watch and laugh. Finally I had enough. When he stopped me one morning and said, 'How,' I said, 'Up your ass, white trash.' For a moment he looked surprised, and then he spit right in my face. It made me so mad I pulled out my pecker and pissed all over his britches. When that white boy looked down and saw that he had Indian piss all over him, he went plumb crazy, then he hit me in the face so hard I thought he'd knocked my head off. But I flew into him like I'd never flown into anyone before. I was getting the best of it, too, until ten of his friends pulled me off and stomped me into the ground like I was a snake. The teacher took me into a room, beat me with a paddle and then kicked me out of school for the rest of the year. When I got home I went out in the marsh alone. I sat on the ground and cried. The more I cried, the madder I got, and I wanted to take a knife and stick a hole in every white skin I could find. But I didn't. If I had, I wouldn't be here now. I would have been blamed again for starting the fight."

Toby had only half listened. He said, "What has all this to do with painting signs?"

Josie reached over, touched Toby's shoulder and said, "Toby, what I mean is that I sometimes feel as you do. I understand. But you're fighting the wind, and no one can fight the wind. You have to bend with it. Even the trees know this."

Toby became pensive, staring across the canal into the darkness of the marsh. "If you do nothing, the wind will blow you away. And already the sawgrass is sending up great clouds of pollen. Are you coming with me or not?"

Josie put the cap back on the bottle and said, "I'll go
with you because I don't have anything else to do. But let
this be the end of it. I'd rather sit here and drink."

They walked back to the table beside the chickee,
and Toby repacked all of the things except the medicine
bag. He put the strap over his neck, and the pouch hung
just below the giant crocodile tooth he already wore.

When they reached the pickup, Toby drove east
toward the Highway 27 junction leading to Miami. Wind
gushed through the open space of the missing windshield. Josie opened the bottle, took a drink and said,
"Toby, are you sure you want to waste our time on
something as useless and foolish as this? There are other
things we could do. We could gig frogs or catch fish. Or
we could sit by the canal and drink."

Toby replied, "They will know the meaning of the
word someday."

It was long after midnight when Toby returned to his
camp. Lucy aroused herself and said sleepily, "Have you
already gigged the frogs?"

"No," he answered softly. "I helped Josie with some
things at the village, and it took longer than I expected.
I'll go now."

"But it's so late. You should stay here and rest."

Toby put the buckskin bundle back into the cabinet
and said, "It's not so late as you think. You've been
asleep. I will go now and be back to you soon. We need
the extra money."

He was far into the swamp before he realized that he
still had the medicine bag around his neck.

SEVEN

J une passed into July and still there was no
rain except for one late-afternoon sprinkle
that succeeded only in making the dust on
Toby's bus run in thin streaks like mascara.

Two days after the sign painting episode, the road
foreman said that some high school students had pulled
a foolish prank and painted an odd word on highway
markers all the way from the Highway 27 junction to
Monroe Station. It angered Toby to know that what he
had done was passed off merely as a prank, and even
worse, he had been made part of a special crew assigned
to take paint remover and clean all of the signs.

Bentley found a windshield for Toby in Naples, and
Toby spent an entire Sunday trying to fit the old, brittle
glass into the frame without breaking it. The windshield
cost fifty dollars, and Bentley accepted ten dollars down
with ten dollars due each Saturday.

Lucy noticed that Toby was spending more and more
time in brooding moods. He would eat his food silently
and then sit alone by the side of the chickee, staring at
something in the distance she could not see. Always
before, they enjoyed long conversations about things that
happened during the day, but now he talked little. She

sensed he did not want to discuss whatever it was that bothered him. She thought she knew, but all she could do was talk whenever he wished to talk and hope that his depressed mood would soon pass.

Each night now he would put on the warrior clothes, sometimes wearing them as he watched the night creep through the cypress trees and invade the clearing. One night he wore the clothes into the swamp. He also spent much time turning the medicine bag over and over in his hands, pressing it gently as if to find its secret power and make it come alive. Lucy watched silently, wishing that his grandfather had never given it to him.

Toby still gigged frogs each night, but the catch was poor and not worth the effort. As the drought continued and the water level dropped, the frogs retreated into the dense sawgrass where they were impossible to find.

In order to make extra money, Toby promised Josie Billie he would wrestle alligators for the tourists a half-day each Saturday. He arose early and arrived at the village while Josie was eating breakfast. With him he had a box containing figures of alligators, herons and deer he had carved from cypress.

Toby sat at the table and drank coffee while Josie finished eating. He took several of the figures from the box and asked, "Are these worth anything, Josie?"

Josie examined one carefully. "These are the best I have seen. Did you carve them?"

"Yes. I sometimes make them at night. Can you sell them?"

"I'm sure we can sell them. The tourists don't spend

their money as quickly now as they used to, but we'll get all we can for them. Maybe fifteen or twenty dollars each. Whatever we get, you'll keep half. How many do you have?"

Toby was pleased by the response. He said, "More than a dozen."

"Leave them in the store. You should do more of this."

"Maybe I will if these sell."

"They will sell. It may take a little time, but we can sell all you make. These are the best I have seen."

Toby asked, "How much are the jackets in the store? I may buy one for Lucy. I haven't been good to her lately."

"From the tourists we get fifty dollars and up. You can have any one on the rack for twenty-five."

"Could you take this out of the carvings when they're sold?"

"Sure. And you'll have extra money coming too. Before you leave, pick out any one you want. This will make a nice gift for Lucy. Have you been mean to her?"

"No, it's not that. I can't really explain it. More and more lately I've been thinking of things in the past. I try not to, but I do. I know it's lonely for Lucy being at the camp alone so much, and she would like to talk at night and see more of me. But I must have the extra money gigging frogs, and when I am at the camp, my mind wanders. I thought maybe the jacket would make her happy."

"They're very nice," Josie said. "They're hand-made by Tanya Gopher and Lillie Jumper, and no one is better than them when it comes to cloth."

"I'll select one before I leave." He then asked, "Who

will wrestle this morning?"

"You and me and Frank Willie. It should be a good day. The tourist traffic has picked up lately."

"I hope we make some money. The truck windshield cost fifty dollars, and I've paid only ten. And soon the rent will be due again."

Josie pushed the plate aside, got up and said, "Well, we better go on down to the pits and warm up the 'gators. The tourists expect a good show for their fifty cents."

At noon they came back to the chickee, and Josie heaped two tin plates with fried chicken. He said, "If I stay in the pit all afternoon, I need a stiff drink. You want one?"

"Yes," Toby replied.

Josie took a bottle from the shelf, poured two tin coffee mugs full, and handed one to Toby. Then they sat at the table. Josie stripped a chicken leg in one bite, threw the bone to a dog and said, "The 'gators seemed to be frisky this morning."

"I noticed that," Toby said. "I'm a little sore. You should have seen the look on a woman's face when I threw a 'gator on his back, rubbed his stomach and made him go limp. I believe she thought I had broken his neck. She shouted for me not to hurt him, and the 'gator was only sleeping."

Josie chuckled. "I have seen women scream and faint while watching. Once when a 'gator grabbed me by the leg, an old man filled his pants. The smell was awful. We had to take him to the chickee and clean him up before he could leave the village. Sometimes the tourists put on a better show than the 'gators."

Toby asked, "Do you know yet how much we made this morning?"

"It wasn't too bad. Your part is seven dollars. Stay this afternoon and you'll make more. The traffic is better in the afternoon."

Toby took a drink of the whiskey. "I am going into the Glades for a few days next week, and I've got a lot of things to do this afternoon."

"Where are you going?"

"First I'll visit Grandfather, and then I don't know where I'll go. Just into the Glades. I'm tired of my job on the road, and I just want to go away for a few days."

"I can't see why you don't quit that kind of work. You could wrestle and carve figures and gig frogs and make enough money to get by."

"Maybe I could quit if the rains come. The gigging isn't good now, and the frogs I get won't even pay for the gasoline I use going and coming from my road job. But with the baby coming, I need a steady job. I have to save money for the baby."

"You could make enough," Josie insisted.

"Maybe," Toby replied. "Someday I may try this. I'll go now and pick out the jacket for Lucy, then I have to get back to the camp."

"You want another drink first?" Josie said.

"One. And then I must go."

Josie refilled the mugs. He said, "I wouldn't work on the roads cutting bushes for anyone. I would rather skin snakes for a living."

When Toby left the village, he stopped a mile up the road at a small chickee on the bank of the drainage canal. Beside the chickee there was a sign, "Willie Tigertail's Airboat Rides — See The Everglades — $2.50 Each."

Willie Tigertail was sitting on a bench beneath the chickee. Toby got out of the pickup, walked over to him and said, "Hello, Willie. How's business?"

"Not too bad, Toby. But if we don't get rain soon, I'll need a jeep or a swamp buggy instead of the airboat. What brings you down this way?"

"I've been wrestling at the Osceola Village this morning. I saw you sitting here and just thought I'd stop for a minute."

Willie frowned. "Well, you can have all that wrestling. I'd rather run an airboat for a living than get in a pit and flop around with a 'gator. You in a hurry?"

"Not too much," Toby said.

"I forgot to bring my lunch, and I need to go get it. Can you watch the airboat? I won't be gone long."

"Yes, I have time to do this."

Willie got up and said, "If anyone comes along before I get back, don't make a trip unless you have at least four. The gasoline's so high now I can't make money with less than that." He walked to his car and drove off.

Toby sat on the bench and shuffled his feet in the dust. The two mugs of whiskey, combined with the heat, were making his head swim. He watched idly as cars raced along the highway in both directions.

One car coming from the east slowed and pulled off the highway, making a crunching sound as the tires bounced over the bed of limestone gravel lining the edge of the road. The car bore an Ohio license plate, and there were two couples inside, both in their fifties.

The driver got out and walked to the chickee. He was dressed in a white knit shirt, blue walking shorts and white canvas shoes, and his arms and face were badly sunburned. He said to Toby, "How much does a ride cost?"

"There on the sign," Toby replied, pointing to the large sign the man had obviously seen. "Two-fifty each."

The man looked briefly at the airboat and then back to Toby. "That's a bit steep just for a ride, isn't it? But I'll tell you what I'll do. How about six dollars for the four of us?"

The question irritated Toby. He said flatly, "It's two-fifty each!"

"Well, I guess we could pay that price. How long does a trip take?"

"About fifteen minutes."

"Could we go now, or do we have to wait for others to fill the boat?"

"You can go now. For the four of you it's ten dollars, and you pay in advance."

The man handed Toby a ten-dollar bill and then motioned for the others to get out of the car. Toby went down to the canal and cranked the airboat engine.

Willie Tigertail's boat was much larger than Toby's. It had five rows of wooden seats and was designed to carry up to fifteen passengers, and it also had a larger and more powerful engine.

Directly across from the landing, a water path

opened into the sawgrass and moved to the north. It made a winding circle two miles into the marsh and came back to the canal a hundred yards south of the landing. The path was eight feet wide and had been used so much that it was totally free of sawgrass. The usual ride was to move along the path dead slow so the tourists could watch the water birds and the small alligators as they poked their snouts out of the sawgrass or from lily ponds along the way.

Toby guided the boat into the path's entrance and moved forward slowly. He had driven the path many times before for Willie Tigertail and knew it well. He shouted over the roar of the engine, "Look close and you will see the alligator!" One of the women shielded her ears from the booming noise of the engine.

When he reached the point where the water path turned south back toward the highway, Toby did not turn with the path. Instead, he shoved the throttle full forward and bounded off over the solid sawgrass with a roar. All of the passengers looked startled, and one woman's straw hat blew off and sailed over the grass.

Toby continued north for two miles with the boat crashing forward at better than fifty miles an hour. Sawgrass smashing into the boat's bow sounded like the sharp pop of firecrackers. Then he turned east toward a mud island. When he reached the island he hit the inclined bank at full speed, causing the boat to shoot upward and become airborne. It sailed for forty feet over the small island and came down with a loud thud in a thick growth of water lilies. The passengers left their seats and tumbled into the bottom of the boat.

One of the men jumped up and shouted, "God-dammit, fellow! What the hell are you trying to do, kill us all?"

Toby tried to suppress a grin that was breaking across his face. He shouted back over the roar of the engine, "It's part of the ride! It's called jumping the 'gator hump!"

"Take this damned thing back where we came from!" the man said angrily, helping his wife back onto the seat. "Now!"

Toby retraced his way back to the water path at no more than five miles an hour, then he finished the ride at dead slow. As soon as the bow of the boat touched the landing, both couples jumped out simultaneously and headed for the car. One man muttered, "Crazy Indian!"

Toby had not finished securing the boat when the car's rear tires screeched wildly, sending a shower of rocks into the canal. He smiled as the car reached the highway and sped swiftly away over the hot asphalt.

Willie Tigertail had driven up just as the car roared away from the landing. He walked to the bench beneath the chickee and said, "What was that all about?"

"They were four tourists I took for a ride. One man said they were in a hurry to get to Naples."

"They must of been," Willie said, scratching his head. "Looks like they dug two ruts right through the rock. Crazy tourists. Always in a hurry."

Toby handed Willie the money. "Well, see you later. I hope business is good this afternoon."

Willie reached into a brown paper bag. "You want a fish sandwich and a beer before you go?"

"No thanks. I ate at the village."

"Well, I sure appreciate this, Toby. Stop by next time you're down this way."

"I will," Toby said, "and I enjoyed the ride. You have a fine boat, Willie. It runs real good."

Toby turned onto the Loop Road at Forty Mile Bend, and when he reached Pinecrest he stopped at the Hughes Store and purchased five pounds of pork chops and two cartons of eggs. Further down the road, as he passed Don Lowry's place, he thought of the night when the strange men had pounded him into the dust.

But even this recollection couldn't dim his high spirits. He was exhilarated with the anticipation of the coming trip into the Glades and of not reporting to work Monday morning.

Toby had not yet told Lucy what he planned to do, but he stopped Friday afternoon on his way home from work and spent half his paycheck at Big Jim Bentley's for twice the amount of supplies he usually brought home. The refrigerator and the shelf were well stocked, and Lucy wondered about his sudden change of appetite.

When he reached the camp Lucy was in the garden, watering a row of tomato plants. He went inside the bus and put the pork chops and eggs into the refrigerator, then he hid the jacket beneath Lucy's pillow on the bed.

Toby then went outside to the grill and poured himself a cup of coffee. Lucy came over to him, immediately aware of his change of mood. She said, "You must have had a good morning at the village. Your eyes are sparkling."

"It wasn't bad. Six women tourists fainted, and two

men went crazy and ran off into the sawgrass behind the pits." He thought of the airboat ride and chuckled. "And I took four tourists on the boat of Willie Tigertail and showed them how to do the 'gator hump jump."

Lucy sat down beside him and said, "You're being silly, Toby. You act like a little boy who has seen his first deer in the woods."

"I've seen many deer." He put his arm around her, pulled her close and said, "There's something for you hidden in the bus."

"Stop teasing me, Toby," she said. "What is it?"

"First, there's something else you must know. I'm not going to work Monday. I'll spend that day and the night with Grandfather, and then I'll stay in the Glades for a few days."

She was not surprised by Toby's words, but now she knew why his mood had changed. Several times in the past he had gone off alone for a few days, and she did not mind. To her this was the natural way of Seminole men. She said, "Have you told this to the road foreman?"

"Yes. I told him yesterday morning. Mr. Simpson said it would be all right. He said he would keep my job open for me if I didn't miss but a few days."

"It was good of him to do that. Steady jobs are hard to find, and there are many others who would like to take your place." She took his hand and said, childlike, "But tell me now, Toby. What is it you've hidden in the bus?"

He enjoyed her eagerness. He said, "Let's go and see."

They walked together to the bus and went inside. Toby said, "I'll give you a clue. It's not in the refrigerator, and it's not something you can eat."

Lucy opened the cabinets and searched them, then she looked along the shelves. She even looked beneath the bed. Finally she said, "Toby, is there really something here?"

He said, "Search the top of the bed."

She immediately grabbed the pillow and found a rainbow of color beneath it. The jacket was patterned after the colors of a tree snail. She picked it up and ran her fingers across the cloth. "It's beautiful," she said, her voice excited. "But I've seen these in the store on the reservation, and I know what they cost. Pappa could never afford to buy one for me, and you shouldn't have spent so much money just to bring me a gift."

"It cost nothing," Toby said, pleased that she liked the jacket. "I left a box of my wood carvings with Josie. He says they are the best he has seen, and he can get fifteen or twenty dollars each from the tourists. I'll get half. When the carvings are sold, Josie will take out the cost of the jacket and I'll still have money coming." He put his hands on her shoulders and said enthusiastically, "Lucy, I could carve at least a dozen of these each week if I did nothing else. That would be as much or maybe more than I make on the road."

She smiled, and then she slipped on the jacket. It was a perfect fit. She said, "Toby . . . I'll love it always. It's the nicest present I've ever known. And I'm happy about the carvings. I always knew they were good. But you've never done this for money. It would mean sitting at the table all day every day. Are you sure this is what you wish to do?"

He knew she was right. He had carved the figures only for pleasure, and maybe he couldn't do so well under the pressure of money. He would continue to carve them only at his own pace. He said, "We'll see. Maybe they wouldn't be so good if I hurry. But I'll carve as many as I can, and they will bring extra money for the baby."

Toby's jubilant mood infected Lucy. She said, "I have fresh okra in the garden, and also peppers and tomato. And there's still turtle meat in the refrigerator. If you will get crawfish I'll make your favorite gumbo. Do you think you can do this?"

His face brightened at the mention of turtle and crawfish gumbo. He said eagerly, "I will get you a bushel. I know where they are plentiful if I can run the 'coons away from them."

She smiled again as she watched him take a bucket from the chickee and trot across the clearing toward the swamp.

After supper Toby drove to Monroe Station and filled the gas cans for the airboat. When he returned, Lucy had finished cleaning the dishes and was sitting at the table beside the chickee. He put the cans down, sat beside her and said, "I must take the gasoline to the airboat. Come and go with me. There is a thing I want you to see."

The sun had sunk below the horizon but was sending fingers of red into the clouds where they were filtered downward, bathing the cypress with a mystic orange glow. A flight of white egrets winging westward looked pink against the darkening sky. Trees and vines changed color constantly as the swamp absorbed the last of the day and prepared for night. Lucy followed Toby along the narrow path as this daily phenomenon created a twilight fairyland. Then they entered the open area leading to Lost Creek.

When they reached the airboat landing, all light was gone, and they were in total darkness. Lucy felt a pang of fear as Toby left her and went down the bank to put the cans in the airboat. She could see nothing, and she was afraid Toby would not be able to find her when he came back up the bank. But he had eyes that could see as well as the panther or the nighthawk, and she was relieved when she felt his hand grasp hers.

Toby led her along a trail that bordered the creek. Frogs were beginning to bellow, and from somewhere in the distance there came the sound of an alligator grunting. Then they turned from the path and walked through a thick forest of cabbage palms, feeling their feet sink into a solid matting of fallen fronds. Soon they came to a small knoll of high land just at the point where swamp merged into the great open marsh.

"We'll sit here," Toby said softly.

Lucy dropped down to the ground and moved close to Toby. She leaned against his shoulder and said, "I can see nothing. Why have we come to this place?"

"It will be only a few minutes, and then you will see."

From far across the black distance there suddenly appeared a small tip of silver. The dim glow moved upward and became larger, and soon a ghostly scene of vast sawgrass flats dotted with palm hammocks emerged from the darkness. There was a slight breeze blowing, causing the sawgrass to sway gently. Drops of moonlight seemed to be catching in the tops of the grass like luminous beads lacing the heads of dancers.

Lucy was spellbound. "It's beautiful," she whispered, as if the sound of her voice might shatter the scene and cause it to vanish.

"When I was a boy this was my favorite time of night," Toby said. "I would slip from the chickee and watch as the moon came up through the palms. I come to this place often when I'm gigging frogs."

Lucy put her hand on his and said, "Toby, we'll go and live on a hammock if that is what you wish. I'll do whatever you want to do."

He pushed her backward to the ground gently and moved close beside her, then he cupped her face in his hands. He said, "No, Lucy. That will never be. I only dream. Out there would be no place for you or the baby. It's a hard life now on a hammock, not like the old days. And soon it will be no more. I'm even afraid for Grandfather."

"If you would be happy, I would go."

She felt his arms move around her, and her eyes closed as his face touched hers. They paid no notice as the full moon gathered strength and invaded the knoll of high ground, and it was past midnight when they returned to the camp.

EIGHT

~~~~~~~~~~~~~~~~~~~~~~~~~~~~

W hen the airboat reached Allapattah
Flats at mid-morning, Toby pulled
the boat onto the shore and walked
quietly along the path leading to the back of the cove.

None of the crocodiles were on the opposite bank,
but he could see the eyes of one protruding from the
water. He squatted behind a cocoplum bush and
watched.

"Where are your friends, old one?" he said. "Are they
in the bushes, waiting for me? Or somewhere down
there with you? Would you like my arm, or a leg, or all
of me? But you will have to catch me first. I'm not so
dumb as you think."

Toby continued to squat, staring at the two eyes just
above the surface of the still water. The crocodile wasn't
creating even a ripple, and it remained motionless as a
coot flew into the cove.

Toby watched with interest as the small black bird
paddled around in circles, dipping its head beneath the
surface in search of food. He said, "You best be careful,
little one. You're getting too close. There's instant death
awaiting you."

The coot popped beneath the surface and came up

three feet in front of the eyes. An explosion suddenly ripped the water as two giant jaws shot upward and clamped over the bird. The coot screamed briefly, then it disappeared downward.

"I told you so, little one," Toby said, watching waves spread across the surface. "I warned you, but you wouldn't listen. And there was nothing I could do for you. Now you're only food in the belly of allapattah."

He watched for a few minutes more, then he got up and went back to the airboat.

From the flats he headed straight toward the hammock of his grandfather. As he approached the island he pushed the throttle back and forth, causing the engine to pop like the sound of cannons. The old man was waiting when he rammed the bow of the boat onto the landing.

Toby hugged his grandfather in greeting, and then his grandfather said, "Many airboats pass this way, but I always know when it is you. No one else rides on such a wave of thunder. It is as if the gods are coming out of the sky."

"I am no god, Grandfather," Toby said. "I only know how to make the engine backfire."

Toby took two packages from the boat and followed his grandfather along the path leading to the camp. When they reached the cooking chickee, Toby put the packages on the table and sat on the bench.

"Would you like coffee?" the old man asked.

"Yes. That would be fine."

They sat at the table and sipped from the steaming mugs. Toby said, "I will stay here with you tonight,

Grandfather, and then I will spend a few days in the Glades before returning home."

"That is good. I will enjoy your company, and we will talk of many things."

"Do you know what I've brought?" Toby asked. "I will tell you. I have five pounds of pork chops and two dozen eggs. We'll have pork chops tonight and eggs in the morning. How does that sound to you?"

The old man smiled. "I have not eaten eggs in more than a year. Do we have to wait until morning? Could we not have some of them tonight?"

"Yes. We'll have eggs tonight with the pork chops. How many can you eat?"

"I will eat six tonight and six in the morning."

Toby laughed. "You have a big stomach for such a slender man, Grandfather. It will be pork chops and eggs tonight, and then I will gig frogs. In the morning we'll have fried legs with our eggs. And I will also make a pot of corn grits. What else would you have?"

"That would be enough," the old man said, still smiling. "Unless you brought some of the cake buns with sugar on top."

"There are two packages of them in the bag. I thought you'd want them. I will get them now."

Toby brought a package of sweet buns back to the table and handed them to his grandfather, then he watched as the old man opened them and ate eagerly. He said, "Would you like to go for a ride in the airboat this afternoon? I have enough gasoline to go from here to Cape Sable if you'd like." He knew his grandfather loved to ride in an airboat.

"That would be fine," the old man replied, smiling again. "But I would not wish to go so far."

"We will go wherever you like, and I will take you on a wave of thunder such as you've never seen or heard."

"Do not make it too loud, Toby. You would frighten away all the rabbits and fish, and then I would have nothing to eat." He suddenly became serious. "Could we go to the hammock of your mother and father and your grandmother? I have wished to visit them lately, but it is too far for the dugout canoe. I am too old now to travel so far with a pole."

"Yes, we will go there," Toby answered. "I haven't seen this ground myself for a long time. We will go as soon as you finish eating."

The fire had burned down to a bed of glowing coals when Toby placed the frying pan on the grill. His grandfather was in the chickee resting from the afternoon's trip. The pork chops sizzled and popped as the pan became hotter. When he finished cooking them he placed the chops on a cypress platter and dropped in the eggs. Biscuits were baking in a Dutch oven on the edge of the grill.

The meal was on the table when Toby beckoned his grandfather. The old man just sat and looked for a moment, and then he ate with relish. Pork chop after pork chop hit his plate until soon there was nothing left but a pile of bones. Then he dipped up the egg yolk with hot biscuits. Toby received more pleasure from watching his grandfather than he did from the meal itself.

When they finished eating they sat on the ground

and leaned back against the trunks of cabbage palms. Night had come completely, and the fire sent flickering shadows around the camp. The old man said, "You are a good cook, Toby. Almost as good as your grandmother. But not quite so good. Do you remember the stews that she made?"

"Yes, I remember," Toby replied. "I could never forget. And I am nothing like her. Anyone can cook pork chops and fry eggs, but I'm glad you enjoyed it. I wish you could eat a meal prepared by Lucy. She is as good as mother or grandmother."

The old man lit his pipe and said, "I am glad you are here, Toby. Many nights now I get lonely."

For a moment Toby thought of again asking his grandfather to come and live in his camp, but he knew this would be useless. He said instead, "Would you like to go with me for a day or so? I would bring you back here on the way home. We will go many places and see many things you haven't seen now for a long time but remember from the old days."

"No, I would not do this," he replied, his voice tired. "I do not go far from the hammock anymore, except to a nearby island to hunt rabbit or spear a fish. I would only be in your way. But when I was as young as you I made many trips. Sometimes we went south to the place where the marsh meets the sea, and it was many days' journey in the dugout canoes. We would come back by the west to the place of many islands, and there we would have great feasts of oysters and clams. And each year we would go to the ocean in the east when the giant turtles crawled onto the sand to lay eggs. One turtle was enough to feed all of the people for many days. And some years we held the Green Corn Dance on the south shore of the great Okeechobee. There were many things there of wonder. The moon vines were so thick they covered the tops of trees, and I often walked on them over the roof of the forest. Keith Huff told me many years ago that it is all gone now. He said the white men have built a giant dike around the lake, and there is nothing left there now but houses and farms. I would not like to see it again. I will stay here on the hammock and remember things as they once were."

Toby got up and said, "I'm going to the airboat and get my gig and lantern, then I will gig frogs for our breakfast."

"There should be many around the shore. I would help you, but I cannot see now in the darkness."

When Toby returned, the old man was still sitting against the tree, but he had slumped forward, sound asleep. The pipe lay at his feet. He did not awaken as Toby picked him up gently and placed him on the palmetto bed beneath the chickee. Toby looked at him for a long time, realizing just how frail he had become. Then he lit the lantern and moved off toward the sound of the croaking frogs.

Toby did not leave his grandfather's hammock until early the next afternoon. They spent part of the morning spearing fish together from the old cypress canoe. Toby still marveled at his grandfather's ability with a lancewood spear. He saw fish Toby could not see, and sometimes he rammed the long shaft downward into

seemingly empty water. But he always brought it back
into the canoe with a flouncing bass attached to the tip.

In late morning they sat at the table drinking coffee
and talking of things in the past, then at noon Toby's
grandfather fried the fish and made a pone of cornbread.
Soon afterward, he was asleep when Toby left. Toby did
not start the airboat engine until he had poled the boat
two miles from the hammock, and then he ran it dead
slow for another mile to lessen the noise.

Toby had no particular destination as he pointed the
boat west and gave it full throttle. His long hair
straightened out as the airboat skimmed through the
sawgrass, stirring up flights of ducks and rails and cor-
morants that hid along his path. When he passed two
miles off the shore of Allapattah Flats, he muttered, "I'll
not stop with you this day, long snouts. I wish no sight
of you today."

He did not slow the airboat until he was well into the
area of the Ten Thousand Islands. Finally he cut the
engine and let the boat drift. Trees on some of the
mangrove islands were white with ibis and snowy egrets,
and the shallows were filled with herons and roseate
spoonbills searching for food. He laughed when two
anhingas engaged in a noisy squabble over a fish one of
them had caught.

He poled the boat into a clump of mangrove trees
and picked oysters from the roots until the bottom of the
boat was covered with shells, then he moved into the
shallows, looking for fish. He finally found an unaware
snook and slammed the gig into its back. When he
cleaned the fish and threw its insides into the water, it

caused a swarm of pelicans to surround the boat, clacking their bills loudly for a handout.

When he left this area he turned south, moving aimlessly again, then he began searching for a place to spend the night. Many of the mangrove islands were inaccessible because of dense barriers of rotted limbs smashed into the water by hurricanes. Once he saw a houseboat anchored in the distance, and he turned away from it.

He finally came to an island with a clear cove. After securing the boat, he gathered wood for a fire. The sun had now dropped low in the sky, and all of the islands were alive with birds seeking a roost for the night. A family of raccoons watched with interest as he brought his supplies ashore, waiting patiently for an opportunity to steal whatever food they could find.

After he built a fire, Toby went back to the shore, stripped naked and waded into the black water. At first it was warm to his body, but as he waded deeper, it became cool. He turned on his back and drifted, looking upward as the sky changed from red to orange. Then he swam back to the shore and put on the faded cut-off jeans.

He threw heaps of oysters into the fire, and when the shells cracked open, he removed them from the fire and scraped off the meat with a knife. It tasted good, and he remembered the times his mother had used oysters in a pot of stew. He then cut the fish into chunks, speared the flesh with a stick and roasted it over the coals. At this moment it seemed to him that all a man ever needed, all there really was to life, was here free for the taking.

The approach of night created a flurry of activity. Flights of birds hurried by over the island, and fish snapped at minnows and bugs on top of the water. For a while Toby sat on the shore by the airboat and watched all of this. Then when the last trace of light was dying, all motion stopped. No living thing moved, and the great marsh became soundless. Even the sawgrass seemed somber, and the palm islands in the distance looked not real but like objects painted onto a giant canvas. Stars and the moon gradually coming into the sky caught his interest momentarily. But suddenly he felt alone.

He thought of the time only two nights ago when he held Lucy in his arms as this same moon drove the darkness from the marsh. He could still smell her and feel her swollen body pressed tightly against him. And then he thought of his grandfather, an old man excited because of a supper of pork chops and chicken eggs, then asleep alone against the trunk of a cabbage palm. There were no longer any children to brighten his campfire, no longer a woman to share life, no companions to exchange tales. And there never would be.

A realization came to Toby that being here on this remote mangrove island was a selfish thing. He could not run forever. He knew that the past was dead, and he would not find it out here or elsewhere. It lay on the hammock with his mother and his father and his grandmother, and soon now his grandfather. He wished he had not left the old man alone. It also bothered him that he was thinking of these things. Always before when he went away alone for a few days, it gave him a feeling of freedom; but now something was different, and he could not understand.

He got up and threw more sticks onto the fire, causing sparks to dance over the dying coals. Then he lay back on the blanket and watched as a jetliner roared through the night, making its way swiftly across the silent marsh toward Miami. The airplane's lights blinked and sparkled like fast moving stars, and soon it dropped below the horizon and was no more.

Toby was not aware when sleep finally came, but it was closer to dawn than to midnight.

The next morning, Toby pointed the airboat eastward. He had intended to make his way south to Whitewater Bay and cut back north from there, but now he headed straight for the hammock of his grandfather.

He did not slow the boat as he passed Allapattah Flats, and the speeding craft bounded across the marsh like a frightened deer. When he approached the hammock, he pushed the throttle back and forth, causing booming backfires to shoot from the engine's exhaust. In the distance, Toby could see his grandfather standing by the landing, waiting.

NINE

Toby stayed with his grandfather for two days and nights, and returned home Thursday afternoon. Lucy was fine, and she was happy to see that Toby seemed relaxed. That night they sat by the chickee, talking about the trip. He carved on a block of cypress as he told her how his grandfather had eaten a dozen eggs in two meals, remarking that perhaps he should take chickens to the hammock.

At dawn the next morning Toby left for his job, but he returned to the camp before noon. He walked from the pickup and sat on the bench beside the chickee.

Lucy came outside, and when she looked at Toby she was alarmed by the dejected expression on his face. She said, "Why are you back so soon? What has happened?"

He spoke angrily, "He gave my job away! Someone else has my job! Mr. Simpson lied to me!"

Lucy sat beside him. "Did he tell you why he did this?"

"He said they had an emergency job to do on a bridge, and he had to have a full crew. He told me to come back in about a month and maybe there would be something open then. But he lied to me! If I had known this would happen, I wouldn't have gone on the trip."

"Maybe it is as he says," Lucy said, trying to calm him. "Maybe he couldn't help what he did."

"He lied to me!" Toby repeated. "The rent's due again, and I still owe Mr. Bentley on the windshield. How much money do we have?"

"I'm not sure." She went into the bus and returned with a coffee can. "We have twenty dollars and some change."

"Then I'll take what we have to Mr. Bentley and ask him to wait for the rest. He has always done this before."

Toby got up, put the money into his pocket and started for the truck. Lucy said, "There are other things you can do, Toby. The job on the road was not all there is."

He replied, "I know. But Mr. Simpson lied to me! He didn't have to do that."

Big Jim Bentley was in the garage shed when Toby arrived at Monroe Station. Toby walked over to him and said immediately, "Mr. Bentley, I don't have all that I owe you this week, and I've lost my job on the road. I can give you ten dollars now and the rest soon. I'll wrestle alligators for the tourists at the Osceola Village."

Bentley leaned against a car fender. "How come you lost your job?" he asked. "Are they cutting back on the crew?"

"No, it's not that. When I went into the Glades for a few days, Mr. Simpson said he would hold my job for me, but he gave it to someone else."

"That's too bad," Bentley said. "But it's O.K. about the money. You know I won't press you. And I'll have some work you can do in about a week. I've got a contract to check over all the swamp buggies at the Everglades Hunting Club. That's about three dozen buggies, and some of them will probably need engine overhauls. I know you can do this kind of work, Toby. You did as good an overhaul on that airboat engine as anyone could do. If you work hard at this job, you can make fifty or sixty dollars a week, and the job will last at least a couple of months. That should pull you out of the hole with a little to spare. I've got to hire someone, and the job is yours if you want it."

"That would be fine," Toby said, greatly relieved. "I will do this, and I thank you. I will work hard as you say. When do I start?"

"Probably a week from next Monday. I'll start getting parts next week. And there's something else you might want to do, too. A couple of men came in here this morning asking about a guide with an airboat. Said they wanted to tour the Glades for a few days. They offered twenty dollars a day for a guide and a boat, and I told them I'd try to find someone. I was going to ask Sam Gopher, but you can have it if you want it. They'll be back here early tomorrow morning."

"What is it they want to do?" Toby asked, interested but having doubts.

"I don't know. I didn't question them. They were in a camper van with a Texas tag, so I guess they're just a couple of tourists wanting to see some of the Glades. But twenty bucks a day isn't bad money for running an airboat, and that tourist money spends just like all the rest."

Ordinarily Toby would not have hired himself to

tourists, but now he needed the money. He said without enthusiasm, "I guess I'll do it. Maybe they'll not wish to stay long. I've already been away from my camp for five days."

Bentley asked, "Where do you keep the airboat now?"

"On Lost Creek, close to the edge of the swamp."

"I'll tell you what, then," Bentley said. "Why don't you just meet them in the morning and leave your pickup here while you're gone? I'm not going to be using my buggy for a few days, so you can take them to the airboat in it from here. Shouldn't take you more than an hour to get to Lost Creek. The men can leave their camper here too, and you can get your truck when you bring the buggy back."

"I will be here in the morning," Toby said as he handed Bentley a ten-dollar bill. "I'll try to have all of the money I owe sometime next week. And I thank you for waiting."

"That's O.K.," Bentley said. "There's plenty of ways to make money if you try."

Toby then went into the store, and with the other money he purchased a bucket of red paint and two cartons of beer. When he returned to the camp he put the beer in the refrigerator, opened one and went out to the chickee. Lucy looked up from the grill and said, "Are you hungry now?"

"No, I'm not hungry. I will eat later."

"What did Mr. Bentley say about the money?"

Toby sipped the beer. "He will wait. And he offered me a job in a week working on swamp buggies. He says

I can make fifty or sixty dollars a week, and the job will last two months or more."

Lucy smiled. She didn't think he would find something so soon, and she was pleased. "That is good, Toby. That's about the same as you made on the road. I knew there would be other things for you to do."

"That is not all," Toby said. "I'm to meet two men at Monroe Station in the morning and be their guide for a few days. It pays twenty dollars a day, and maybe with this we can pay some of the rent."

"How did you come to get this?" she asked curiously.

"Mr. Bentley arranged it." Toby got up, went into the bus and returned with his hunting knife and a block of cypress. "I am going to carve a crocodile," he said, "but this one I will make for the baby."

Lucy sat beside him and said, "I knew things would work out, Toby."

"We'll be fine," he replied. "But Mr. Simpson didn't have to lie to me."

TEN

The brown camper van was parked beside the building when Toby arrived at the store the next morning. When he went inside, there were two men seated at a table, eating ham and eggs and drinking beer. Toby said to them, "Are you the ones who need a guide?"

The two men studied Toby carefully. One said, "Yeah, that's us. I'm Jesse Thornton and this is Carl Avery. We're from Texas. What's your name?"

"Toby. Toby Tiger."

"Tiger?" The man chuckled. "Now that's a good old Irish name. You know these swamps well?"

"I've known them all my life. I was born in the marsh."

"That's good," Thornton said. "We just want to poke around a bit out there and see if you've got anything here we don't have back in Texas. We've heard this place is kind of weird, and we want to see."

"I can take you wherever you wish," Toby said.

"Fifteen a day O.K. with you?" Thornton asked, assuming the role of spokesman for the two.

For a moment Toby was perplexed, then he said, "Mr. Bentley said it would be twenty dollars a day including my airboat."

"Well, if that's what he told you, O.K. It's a deal. We don't want to cheat anyone. And maybe we'll give you a little something extra if you show us a good time."

The two men got up. Both were in their middle forties, and both were more than six feet tall and heavy built. They wore gray hunting clothes and high-topped leather boots.

As they followed Toby outside, Toby said, "We'll go from here to Lost Creek in the swamp buggy, then we will go into the Glades in my airboat."

"Good," Avery said. "We didn't come down here to go hikin'. We could of done that in Texas. We'll get our things from the camper."

Toby went behind the building and put two cans of gasoline into the buggy. When the two men came around the side of the garage, they both carried large canvas packs and .270 rifles. Toby took the packs and put them into the back of the buggy.

Thornton looked curiously at the huge airplane tires on the small vehicle. He said, "Will this thing go through water? It ought to float with them tires."

"It will go anywhere in the swamp," Toby said, "but we won't run through much water. The swamp is very dry now."

Toby got behind the wheel and cranked the engine, then the two men climbed in beside him and they headed south.

For several miles Toby ran parallel to the Loop Road. The land here was mostly open and dotted with dwarf cypress. In normal times the ground would have been

mushy with a thin covering of water, but now the buggy
was leaving a dust trail.

For a while the two men studied the landscape with
interest, and then they became bored. Avery said to
Toby, "Is this all there is out here? I thought this was
supposed to be a swamp."

"We're not really in the swamp yet," Toby replied. "It
won't be long now."

Thornton looked over at Toby and asked casually,
"You a full-blooded Seminole?"

"Yes. My parents and my grandparents and those
before them have lived on this land." He thought of telling them of the warrior clothes that had been passed
down to him but decided against it.

Thornton then said, "Well, we don't have Seminoles
in my part of Texas so far as I know, but we've had about
every other kind of Indian at one time or another. Most
of the Indians left in Texas are good Indians. They're
planted six feet under the ground." Thornton and Avery
both laughed, and then Thornton said, "No offense,
fellow. Just an old Texas joke, that's all."

Toby said nothing.

When they crossed the Loop Road, the swamp
became thicker, and several times they ran through
stretches of shallow water. Toby could no longer drive in
a fairly straight line. He had to weave the buggy around
thick growths of trees and vines, and twice he had to
backtrack and find another way.

Avery suddenly said, "Jesus, fellow, stop this thing a
minute!" He was slapping at his arms and neck. "How
the hell can you stand skeeters like this? I got to put

something on before they suck·the blood out of me."

Toby stopped the buggy beneath a thick clump of pond cypress. He had paid no heed to the mosquitoes. "They will not be so bad when we reach the open Glades," he said.

Avery opened one of the packs, took out a can of repellent and sprayed himself, then he handed it to Thornton. "You want a drink?" he asked.

"Yeah, I could use one," Thornton replied.

While Avery was taking a bottle of whiskey from the pack, Thornton suddenly threw up his rifle and fired. The unexpected explosion startled Toby. He looked up quickly and saw a large raccoon fall from a limb and hit the ground with a thud.

"Got him!" Thornton exclaimed excitedly.

The high-caliber rifle had knocked half the raccoon's head off. Toby watched as blood gushed from the small animal and stained the ground. He said, "Do you want the 'coon for your supper? If you do, I will clean it."

"Are you kiddin'?" Thornton said, staring at Toby. "Me eat a 'coon? Back where we come from, that's nigger food. I was just testin' my sight."

Both men took deep drinks from the bottle, then Toby cranked the engine and moved forward again. He soon reached Lost Creek and parked the buggy on the bank beside the airboat.

Toby loaded the gas cans and packs into the boat, and then the two men climbed in. He said, "Where is it you wish to go?"

"Anywhere you want to take us," Thornton replied. "You're the guide. We're just along for the ride."

When he reached the marsh, Toby gunned the engine and headed south. The boat was overloaded and couldn't reach top speed, so he cruised steadily at about twenty-five miles an hour, circling several hammocks before he turned west. Thornton then motioned for him to stop, and he pulled back on the throttle.

Thornton said, "What's on them little islands?"

Toby replied, "Some have nothing, and some have deer and rabbit."

"Let's go in and have a closer look," Thornton said.

Toby guided the boat to a small hammock and circled at dead slow. Several coots popped in and out of clumps of pickerel weed, and a few egrets rested in trees. A great blue heron walked slowly along the shore, pecking at the bottom with its long beak. Avery threw up his rifle and fired, then the giant bird toppled forward into the shallow water and lay still.

Toby shook his head. He said, "The heron is no good to eat. If you want bird, we'll have to find ducks. But it's out of season now for all game."

"We got food in the packs," Avery said. "If we want to shoot ducks, we can do that in Texas. I never got a crack at one of them big birds before."

Thornton said, "Is this whole place nothin' but grass and islands? I've had about enough of this already. We want to see somethin' different."

Toby thought for a moment, and then he said, "Would you like to see crocodiles?"

"Are you kiddin'?" Thornton exclaimed. "You'd have to take us to Africa for that."

"There are a few left here," Toby said.

"Crocodiles?" Thornton questioned again.

"Yes. There are but a few left. Would you like to see them?"

"Sure," Thornton replied. "How far is it?"

Toby said, "They live on Allapattah Flats, only a short distance from here."

"Well, then, let's have a look," Thornton said, still doubtful.

Toby gave the engine full throttle, and he soon guided the boat ashore at the island. When the two men got out he said to them, "You must be very quiet and very careful. Crocodiles are dangerous. They are not like alligators."

Toby guided them along the narrow path to the back of the cove. Only one crocodile was on the opposite bank. He said quietly, "This is their den, and no one but me knows they are here. There are also three others."

Both men stared across the water. Thornton exclaimed, "Well I'm damned! It is a croc. I've seen pictures of them with that pointed snout."

Before Toby realized what was happening, Thornton put three bullets into the crocodile's head. The croc jumped backward as the first bullet shattered its brain, and then it lay still.

For a moment Toby just stared, not believing what he had seen. Then the sight of the lifeless body pumping blood down the bank brought reality to what he witnessed. Anger boiled within him, and he shouted, "You've killed him! You've killed him for nothing! There were only four, and now you've killed one for no reason!"

Thornton and Avery were startled by Toby's unexpected outburst. Thornton stepped back and said, "Now just cool down a bit, fellow. Don't blow your cork. You think I could pass up a chance like this? Something like this is what we came here for."

Toby repeated, "You've killed him for nothing! There were only four! I shouldn't have brought you here!"

Thornton then disregarded Toby and turned to Avery. He said, "We'll skin him out and slip the hide back to the camper. Can you imagine what they'll say back home when they see this souvenir?"

Toby wanted to grab the rifle and smash the butt into Thornton's face, but he knew instantly that that would be a foolish act. He steadied his trembling hands and said as calmly as possible, "That wouldn't be a wise thing to do. To kill a crocodile or an alligator is a felony. If you're caught with the hide you will be in deep trouble, and you could spend much time in jail for this. It would be best to leave him here now, wait on a nearby hammock, and come back tonight. Then we can skin the crocodile and take the hide out in the darkness."

"That makes sense," Thornton said, impressed by Toby's warning of a prison sentence for what he had done, and also glad that Toby had calmed himself. "When we get that croc hide back to the camper, it'll mean an extra hundred dollars for you." He felt sure that money would close Toby's mouth and gain his cooperation in getting the hide back to Monroe Station.

They followed Toby back to the airboat, then he cranked the engine and headed south. For two miles he ran the boat as fast as it would go, and then he pulled into a large hammock.

Toby picked up the two packs and carried them to a small clearing beneath cabbage palms. He put them down and said, "We will stay here until dark. I must go now and secure the boat."

The two men sat on the ground beside the packs. Thornton opened one, took out a bottle and said, "Man, I could sure use a drink after that. This trip was worth it after all." He turned up the bottle and drank deeply.

Toby walked back to the airboat, shoved it out as far as it would go and cranked the engine. He rammed the throttle forward and gained full speed instantly. When he was a half mile out, he looked back and could see the two men on the shore, waving their arms wildly.

It was mid-afternoon when Toby reached Monroe Station. He parked the swamp buggy and started toward his truck. Bentley came from the garage and said, "How come you're back so soon, Toby? And where are the two men?"

"They decided to camp for a few days on a hammock," Toby answered. "I'll go back for them Tuesday."

Bentley said, "They must be some kind of nuts, wanting to spend that much time on a hammock. Well, it takes all kinds, and they all show up out here sooner or later. You can use the buggy when you need it to go after them."

Toby said nothing more as he got into the pickup and drove off. When he reached his camp he told Lucy the same thing he had told Bentley, that the men wanted to camp for several days on a hammock.

For several minutes after the airboat disappeared from sight, Thornton and Avery stared across the silent sawgrass in disbelief. Finally Thornton bellowed, "Dammit to hell! That fool Indian must be loco!"

His booming voice caused a swarm of egrets to flap out of a dwarf cypress and rush away from the hammock.

Avery said, "He was really pissed off about you shootin' the crocodile, but I thought the offer of extra money would buy him. I didn't think he would pull something like this on us. What do we do now?"

"What the hell you think we'll do," Thornton shot back irritably. "We'll walk, that's what! All the way back to the camper. There ain't no bus line runnin' out here, stupid!"

Avery resented the outburst Thornton directed to him, and he said coolly, "What about the equipment?"

"We'll leave it. We can't carry it across the marsh. Could be we might even have to swim some. When we get back to the camper we'll hire someone else to bring us back out here and pick it up."

The two men placed the packs and rifles against the base of a palm. Thornton said, "Strap your knife to your belt. We'll go back to that place and skin out the croc. If we can't drag the hide out with us, we'll pick it up when we come after the packs."

As they left the hammock and waded into the sawgrass, both were surprised by the shallow depth of the water. It came only to their knees. But the sharp blades of sawgrass cut through their clothes and made thin slashes in their flesh, and it seemed to them to be an almost impenetrable barrier. Both men cursed constantly as they made their way foot by foot to the north.

It was late afternoon when they finally reached Allapattah Flats and climbed up the bank to the cove. Only the one dead crocodile was in sight. The two men rolled it onto its back and rammed their knives into the tough hide.

Thornton said, "I've never tried to skin out anything like this. He's sure a tough cuss, ain't he?"

Avery struggled with his knife. "I'll say. What we need is a hatchet or an axe, or maybe even a chain saw."

When finally they succeeded in slicing open the stomach, sweat was pouring from both of them. Avery wiped his brow, smearing blood over his face. He said, "Man, I quit! At this rate it'll take us a week to skin this thing. We better get on out of here and bring something back with us besides these knives."

"I guess you're right," Thornton agreed. "This is a bigger job than I thought it would be."

Avery went down to the cove to wash his hands and face. As he splashed the water he did not notice the two eyes just off the bank. Horror twisted his face as the giant jaws burst suddenly from the still water, grabbed his arm and jerked him headlong into the cove. He screamed once before his body was pulled beneath the surface.

Thornton wheeled around quickly. At first he didn't realize what was happening. Then as he stared into the cove in puzzlement, Avery's thrashing body broke the surface. The crocodile shook him violently and pulled him under again. Thornton's flesh turned white, and his hands trembled. He felt hot vomit rush through his throat and pour out. He tried to scream but could make no sound. Finally he grabbed a stick and started beating the ground hysterically.

ELEVEN

The next morning Toby drove to the Osceola Village to tell Josie he would wrestle alligators for the next week. Josie was in the large pen behind the pits, feeding garfish to the alligators. He came outside when he saw Toby.

As they walked to the wall surrounding one of the pits, Toby said, "I'll wrestle for the next week if you need me."

"We always need you," Josie said, pleased with the news. "But what of your job on the road?"

"When I went into the Glades for a few days, the foreman gave it to someone else."

"That's the best thing that could happen," Josie said. "You don't need to work on the road. Now you can come here all of the time."

"I'm going to start working for Mr. Bentley at Monroe Station a week from Monday. I will fix swamp buggies, and he says I can make fifty or sixty dollars each week."

"That's not bad money," Josie said, "but you can come here any time you wish. The trade has slowed lately, though. Maybe the tourists don't want to stop in this heat."

"Have you sold any of the carvings yet?" Toby asked.

"We sold all of them. One woman even bought four. But we could only get ten dollars each. There were thirteen, so taking out for the jacket, you still have forty dollars coming. Maybe next time we can get more."

"That's good enough," Toby said, disappointed at the price but glad they had been sold. "Now I can pay the rest of the money for the windshield, but I'm still short for the rent."

Josie said, "If you would move here and live in the village, there would be no rent."

Toby thought of what happened with the two men and the crocodile. He said, "I couldn't stand the white tourists that much. I'd rather live on the Loop and pay rent."

Josie asked, "Are you going to stay today and wrestle?"

"Yes."

"Then you can have first turn. The 'gators are always mean during the first show, and you can handle them better than anyone else."

It was late afternoon when the last group of tourists left the village and the wrestling was ended for the day. Toby and Josie were both tired as they walked to the chickee. Josie took a bottle from the shelf inside the chickee, and then they sat at the table. Josie said, "Do you want food? There's a big pot of spare ribs on the grill."

"I'm not hungry now," Toby replied wearily. He poured a mug full of whiskey and downed it in one gulp. He had not eaten at noon either, and he immediately felt the bite of the whiskey in his empty stomach.

Josie said, "Well, I'm hungry, and I'm not so tired I can't eat." He got himself a heaping plate of ribs and then came back to the table.

Toby poured another mug of whiskey, and as he sipped it he became thoughtful. He said, "I saw a bad thing yesterday."

"What was that?"

"Two men hired me as a guide. They were tourists from Texas. I took them to Allapattah Flats, and one of them killed a crocodile."

Josie stopped eating. "Killed a croc?" he questioned. "Why would he do that? You can't sell a hide anymore without going to jail."

"He did it for no reason — just to kill it. And they also shot a raccoon and a heron. After the crocodile was killed, I took them to a hammock south of the flats and left them there."

"You left them on a hammock?"

"Yes."

Josie shook his head. "Well, you'd best not be around when they return. That's a long trek through the sawgrass and the swamp." He dismissed this news from his mind and started eating again. "How was your trip into the Glades?" he asked.

"I didn't go far like I planned. Instead of going south, I spent most of the time with Grandfather." Toby finished the drink and poured another. He continued, "I'm worried for him, Josie. He has become very frail. I think he eats nothing anymore but a fish now and then, and he won't go more than a mile from the hammock. There is no game left out there for him to hunt. I try to take him all the food I can afford, but I am still worried. He shouldn't be out there alone."

"Could he not live at your camp?" Josie asked.

"I have asked this of him many times and he won't even speak of it. You would have to tie him with ropes to get him off that hammock."

Josie threw several bones on the ground and watched as two dogs fought over them. He said, "Well, you can't tell an old man what to do. It's his life. But it is a bad thing to be out there alone in the marsh at his age."

Toby drank again from the mug, and then he said, "He wouldn't be alone out there if they hadn't built the airport in the swamp. When they told us we must leave, my grandmother didn't eat or sleep for many days. She would only sit around the chickee, grieving and saying nothing to anyone. Then she became ill. It was a long trip to the new hammock, and we hadn't been there a month before she died. They killed her for the airport, and the airport ended up as nothing."

"You can't be sure of this, Toby," Josie said. It worried him that Toby even had such thoughts. "Was she not old when you left the land?"

Toby replied, "You can't be sure of anything anymore. But she was not ill before they built the airport and ran us away from the land. They killed her for no more reason than the men killed the crocodile. It was for nothing."

Toby was feeling the whiskey. He started to ask Josie for food but changed his mind and said, "I am going to do another thing tonight. I have thought of it much lately, and I will need your help."

"What is it this time?" Josie asked curiously, noticing also that Toby was drinking more than usual without eating.

"I am going to paint 'allapattah' on the airport runway."

Josie sighed with exasperation. "Toby, you have to be kidding me. Why would you do this? We did it once before with the highway signs, and it meant nothing."

"It will mean something someday."

"Even if you're foolish enough to do this, you can't get into the airport at night with the gate locked."

"I have a hacksaw in the truck. Also the paint."

Josie poured himself a cup of whiskey and downed it quickly, then he went to the grill and came back with a plate of ribs. "Eat this, Toby," he insisted. "And then if you still want to do this foolish thing, I will go with you — but only to keep you out of trouble. I can see no sense in this. Maybe it is only the whiskey."

"It is not the whiskey!" Toby said harshly, pushing the plate back across the table. "This is a thing I must do, a warning to them, and they will know the meaning some-day. If you don't come with me I will go alone."

Josie realized he couldn't convince Toby otherwise, and he knew from Toby's voice that he would do this thing alone. He said, "I will go with you. I don't wish to, but I will. I will go only to keep you out of trouble if I can. Sometimes I think you are crazy to even have such things in your mind."

Toby made no response. Then they walked to the front of the souvenir store. At night there was little traffic on the Trail. Josie looked at the empty highway and said,

"I will drive the truck, but I'll do none of the painting. If you wish to paint a silly word on a strip of concrete, that is your affair."

"I will do the painting alone," Toby said. He took the medicine bag from a paper sack inside the truck and put it around his neck.

They drove west for several miles, and just before they reached the airport gate, Josie pulled to the side of the highway and stopped. He turned off the headlights and said, "I'll wait here. If someone passes and sees you cutting the lock, run back to the truck. I'll keep the motor going."

Toby got out and walked along the edge of the highway. The moon had not yet come up, and he had to feel his way slowly to the gate. No cars passed as he sawed off the lock and swung the gate open. Then he walked back to the truck.

Josie drove the pickup through the gate and along the road leading to the airstrip. The road had been built wide enough to accommodate heavy passenger traffic to and from an international facility which never came into being. It was flanked by a row of tall lamp posts without bulbs. Josie kept the headlights off and drove in darkness. He said to Toby, "If we're seen by a guard, I am going to come out of here so fast it will sling the pistons out of this old truck."

Toby said, "No one will see us if we're careful, and there may not even be guards in here at night. I don't know. But the medicine bag will protect us."

"I'd rather depend on the truck engine than that bag of junk," Josie retorted.

It was an eerie feeling to Josie driving along a super road leading to nowhere in the heart of a black swamp. He had a strong impulse to turn back, but he knew Toby wouldn't allow this. He moved the truck forward slowly, straining his eyes to see through the darkness.

The road cut to the east before it reached the open area of the runways. Toby said, "I have seen this place in the daytime. There is a meadow to the north. Go that way and we'll enter a runway.

Josie left the asphalt road and cut across open ground. It seemed to him that he was driving through a pond of ink, and he expected at any moment to crash into a tree. He said, "I can't see anything, Toby, and I don't know where we are. How can you paint a sign in such darkness?"

"The moon is coming up now. I will be able to see well enough."

Josie finally felt the wheels of the pickup touch concrete. He stopped and said, "Is this far enough?"

"This will do fine. We're near the end of the runway."

Josie cut the engine as Toby took the bucket of paint and a brush from the truck. Josie said, "Hurry with this foolishness, Toby. I want to leave this place."

The moon came up just enough to cut the darkness, but Josie still couldn't understand how Toby could see well enough to paint. He remained in the truck and could distinguish only a dim shadow as Toby smeared red paint across the concrete strip.

Toby was half finished when a row of blue lights flanking both sides of the runway suddenly came on. Josie jumped from the truck and shouted, "What is this thing, Toby? Why have they turned on the lights?'"

Toby stopped the brush and listened to the roar of a jet approaching from the north. He turned to Josie and said, "I'm not finished. It will only take a minute or so more."

Josie said urgently, "Let's get out of here, Toby! Let's get out of here now!"

Toby continued to paint as the roar became louder, not looking up until the airplane's landing lights flooded the edge of the swamp. The jet came in fifty feet over the top of the truck and then suddenly pulled up. The sound of the straining engines was deafening as the huge airplane stopped its downward glide and slowly moved upward again.

Josie fell to the ground and watched as the landing lights bathed the runway to the south. As Toby jumped up and ran for the truck, his foot struck the bucket of red paint, sending it tumbling across the runway. Paint sloshed across his shoe.

Josie had already started the truck forward when Toby jumped onto the running board and climbed inside. They both remained silent as the old pickup shot through the darkness of the meadow and finally reached the asphalt road leading back to the highway. Josie looked back and could see a red flashing light far behind him. He pushed the accelerator to the floor and it sounded as if the engine would come out of the truck. When he reached the gate he slammed on the brakes, sending the pickup screaming sideways onto the Trail. He was three miles down the highway before he finally turned on the headlights.

When they reached the village, Josie stopped in front of the souvenir store. He cut off the engine and the lights, then he slumped forward against the steering wheel and said, "Toby, we are both as crazy as that old bull 'gator in heat! I will never do this thing again! Don't even ask me! Do you understand?"

"It was close," Toby said calmly. "For a minute I thought the airplane would land in the back of the truck. But the medicine bag kept us safe."

"Medicine bag, hell! Did you see the flashing red light coming after us? If they had caught us in there, I don't know what they would have done to us. But it would have been something bad, you can count on that. I will not do this again! Never! They are not going to put me in a cage because of a silly sign."

"I won't go there again myself," Toby said.

Josie became calmer. "Do you want a drink before you go?" he asked.

"No. I have had enough, and I should have eaten. I will get food as soon as I reach the camp."

Josie opened the door and got out. He said shakily, "Well, I am going to the chickee and get myself as drunk as a squirrel eating cocoplum nuts. I will see you in the morning."

Toby cranked the engine and turned on the headlights. He waited until Josie disappeared into the village before driving onto the highway.

TWELVE

~~~~~~

It was early Monday afternoon when Thornton limped across the meadow behind the store at Monroe Station. Big Jim Bentley was inside, eating a plate of bar-b-que and drinking a beer.

When Thornton entered the cafe, Bentley was startled by his appearance. His pants were in shreds, and his legs covered with cuts made by sawgrass. Arms, neck and face were solid mosquito welts.

Thornton slammed his fist onto a table and bellowed wildly, "Where is he?"

Bentley stopped eating. "Where is who?" he asked, puzzled as to why Thornton was even there.

"You know damned well who! That goddam Indian!"

Bentley still didn't understand. He said, "You mean Toby Tiger?"

"Yes, dammit! Where is the bastard?"

Bentley shoved the plate away and stood up. He said, "Now just calm down a bit, fellow. What's this all about? Toby came back here Saturday afternoon and said you wanted to camp on a hammock for a few days and that he'd pick you up Tuesday. I haven't seen him since then."

"He ran off and left us out there!" Thornton exploded. "He left us on a hammock, and I've been walkin' for two days tryin' to find my way out of that goddam swamp! I'm goin' to put the law on him! And if I find him first, I'm goin' to put some fist in his teeth!"

Bentley became even more perplexed. He knew Toby Tiger would never abandon anyone in the marsh without reason. He said, "Did he steal something from you?"

"No," Thornton answered. "He didn't steal anything; but our equipment is lost."

Bentley then said, "Did he take your money as a guide and then run off and leave you?"

"No. We were goin' to pay him when we got back."

Bentley picked up the can, took a drink of beer and said, "Well, if he didn't steal anything, and if you didn't pay him, what's he done to break the law?"

Thornton became even angrier. He said, "He's a murderer, that's what! He left us on an island full of crocodiles, and two of them attacked us! I shot one, but the other one killed Carl! That Indian is a goddam murderer!"

"What?" Bentley exclaimed, wondering if he had actually heard the accusation. "You mean to tell me your friend's been killed by a crocodile?"

"That's right!" Thornton snapped. "I saw it with my own eyes. The crocodile killed him and ate him."

To Bentley the whole scene was becoming ridiculous. He said, "I don't believe that for a second! There's no way that two grown men armed with high-powered rifles can stand on a piece of open ground and let one man be killed and eaten by a croc. No way! You tell that tale to someone around here and they'll laugh you right out of the county."

Thornton bristled. "Are you callin' me a liar?"

"Yes, I'm calling you a liar! When they attacked you — if they attacked you — why didn't you just shoot them?"

For a moment Thornton didn't answer, and then he said, "They came out of the bushes like lightnin'. Carl didn't have time to shoot, and after I killed the first one, my gun jammed. I couldn't do nothin' but stand there and watch."

"You sure they didn't jump down on top of you from out of a tree?" Bentley asked. "If the gun jammed, let's have a look at it and see what's wrong."

"I lost it comin' out of the swamp." Thornton's face again flushed with anger, and he said, "What the hell you mean questionin' me anyway? You're just takin' up for that goddam Indian. Now tell me where he lives!"

"His camp is about ten miles down the Loop Road, but he won't be there now. He's working this week at the Osceola Village on the Trail."

Thornton said, "Well, I'm goin' to put the law on him, and if the law won't do nothin', I will! Back where I come from we know how to handle something like this. I got a forty-four pistol out there in the camper. I'll put some hot lead in his guts, and that's a fact! I'm goin' to leave now, but I'll be back!"

The words angered Bentley, and he said harshly, "You sure are going to leave! We know how to handle things out here too. It's a swamp game we play called 'gator stomp, and I've been champion for the past five years. And that's a fact! Now you get the hell out of here before

I stomp a mudhole in you and then bounce you around the walls like a hickernut!"

Thornton stormed out. Bentley went to the door and watched as he got into the camper and drove off hurriedly toward Naples, then he went back to the table. He scratched his head absently, trying to make some sense from all of this.

Just before dark, Toby stopped at Monroe Station on his way home from the Osceola Village. When he entered the store, Bentley was sitting on a counter in the grocery section. Toby walked up to him and said, "Mr. Bentley, I have the rest of the money for the windshield, but I can pay only ten dollars on the rent. Here's fifty dollars, and I will pay more by this weekend."

Bentley took the bills, put them into his pocket and said, "You make all this wrestling 'gators?"

"No. Most of it came from wood carvings I sold, but I also made some wrestling. I would have come by and paid you last night but I was late getting back from the village."

"That's good, Toby," Bentley said. "I know you'll clear this up before long. You'll make good money fixing the buggies, and things'll work out O.K. for you."

Toby took a five-dollar bill from his pocket, handed it to Bentley and said, "I need a gallon of milk, two loaves of bread and a pound of bacon."

Bentley put the things into a paper bag and then handed Toby his change. He said, "By the way, Toby, a man was in here this afternoon looking for you."

"Who was that?"

"One of those fellows you took out in the Glades. Thornton. Seems they didn't really want to camp on a hammock. When Thornton came in here he looked like he'd been in a pit full of wildcats."

Toby had started to pick up the package but stopped. "He was here?" he asked.

"Yeah, he was here. And I ain't never seen a man madder than him. He claimed you just dumped them on a hammock and took off. He also told me a wild tale about you leaving them on an island full of crocodiles. Said his partner, Avery, was killed and eaten by a croc."

Toby was shocked by the words. He said, "That's not true, Mr. Bentley. I left them two miles from Allapattah Flats. What he says isn't possible. There are no crocodiles anywhere now but at Allapattah Flats, and I didn't leave them there."

Bentley looked straight into Toby's eyes and said, "What happened out there, Toby? I know Thornton didn't tell me the truth, and I don't think you've told me everything either."

"They were bad men," Toby said, knowing that he must tell Bentley exactly what happened. "In the swamp they killed a raccoon for no reason, and later they shot a heron. I took them to Allapattah Flats, and there Thornton killed a crocodile. There were only four left, and he killed one for no reason but just to kill. It was after this that I left them on a hammock two miles from the flats."

"He killed a croc?" Bentley questioned.

"Yes. They were going to bring the hide back here after dark and put it in the camper. They offered me a hundred dollars to help. I took them to the hammock to wait until night before skinning the crocodile, then I left them there."

"Well I'm damned!" Bentley exclaimed. "No wonder he made up such a lie. He probably knows he's committed a felony. They must have gone back to the flats to skin the croc, and whatever happened, it happened there. But why didn't you just come on back here and report them to the law?"

"I thought what I did was best."

Bentley said, "He said he was going to put the law on you for this, and I'm sure he will. You'll hear more from this before it's over, but I don't think you're in any trouble because of it. If the truth is found out, then Thornton will be the one in hot water. But he also threatened to kill you, so when you're around him again, Toby, be careful."

"I didn't mean them harm," Toby said. "But they did bad things. They killed without reason."

As Toby started to pick up the package, Bentley said, "Something else I wanted to mention, Toby. One of the guards who works a night shift down at the airport stopped in here early this morning for breakfast on his way to Ochopee. He said somebody busted in down there last night and dumped a bucket of red paint on a runway. That's all they did, just dump paint and make a few letters. This guy said nobody down there could figure out why the hell anybody would do that, unless it was some high school kids pulling a prank. But they almost got hit by a jet making a practice landing."

Toby gripped the sack, suddenly wanting to get out

of the store quickly. Bentley then said, "That paint
sounded like the same kind somebody used to paint an
Indian word all over the highway signs not long ago. I
know you've been painting some cabinets or something
for Lucy inside the bus, but you better clean that red
paint off your shoe. Somebody might get the wrong idea."

Toby looked down at his shoe. He stammered, "Mr.
Bentley . . . I don't know how that paint got there . . .
I must have . . ."

Bentley interrupted, "Toby, if you ever want to talk
about anything that's bothering you, I'm a good listener.
We all have to look out for each other here in the swamp.
If we don't, nobody will. I'm just a dumb old coot and
I know it, but sometimes I can help. You hear?"

Toby said, "Yes, Mr. Bentley, I hear. And I will clean
the shoe as soon as I get to the camp." Then he turned
and walked quickly from the store.

THIRTEEN

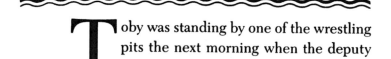

Toby was standing by one of the wrestling pits the next morning when the deputy sheriff and Thornton entered the village. As soon as Thornton recognized Toby, he exclaimed loudly, "That's him! He's the one!"

Josie walked over and stood by Toby as the two men approached. The deputy said, "Are you Toby Tiger?"

"Yes," Toby answered, expecting this would happen.

"Have you seen this man before?"

"Yes. He hired me last week as a guide."

"How many men were there?"

"There were two. This one and another."

The deputy then said, "Thornton here has a pretty wild tale about you leaving them someplace where there were crocodiles, and about his friend being killed by a croc."

"Yes, I know," Toby said. "Mr. Bentley at Monroe Station told me last night. But what this man says is not true. I didn't leave them where there were crocodiles."

"I told you he'd lie about it!" Thornton snapped, stepping toward Toby. "I told you, didn't I?"

"Now just a minute, Thornton," the deputy said, stepping between Thornton and Toby. "Simmer down and let me handle this." He turned back to Toby. "Let's hear your side of what happened."

Toby said, "I took them to Allapattah Flats to see the crocodiles. This man killed one of them. They were going to skin out the hide and take it back to their camper, and they offered me a hundred dollars to help. I told them they would be in deep trouble if caught with the hide, that it would be better to wait until after dark. Then I took them to a hammock two miles away. After I had taken their gear into a clearing I went back to the airboat and left them. I did this because I wanted no part of what they had done. But there has never been a crocodile at the place where I left them."

"That's a damned lie!" Thornton exploded. "I ought to knock the livin'. . ."

"That's enough!" the deputy said, grabbing Thornton's arm. Several Indians in the village came forward to watch the commotion. The deputy then said to Thornton, "How the hell do you think I'm going to find out what happened if I don't ask questions? Now you calm yourself down and keep it that way!"

"He's lyin'!" Thornton repeated.

"We'll see about that," the deputy said. "We'll go out there where this happened and see what we can find." He turned to Toby. "You got a place here where I can launch my airboat?"

"There's a landing just behind the village," Toby replied.

"I'll bring the car and trailer around there," the deputy said. "You two wait at the landing."

Toby said to Josie, "I'll see you later."

"Is there anything I can do?" Josie asked, concerned for Toby.

"No. There is nothing."

Toby helped the deputy slide the airboat off the trailer and into the canal. The deputy took a .44 magnum rifle from the patrol car, and then they all got into the boat. The engine thundered to life, and the deputy guided the boat along a narrow creek. When they reached the sawgrass he shoved the throttle forward, and the airboat dashed away quickly.

It took them an hour to cross the marsh, and when they approached the area of Lost Creek, Toby pointed the way to Allapattah Flats. Soon the deputy guided the boat ashore at the island, and they all got out.

Toby led them along the path to the cove. The dead crocodile was on the opposite bank, lying on its back, and another crocodile was asleep just to the left of the carcass.

The deputy said to Thornton, "Well, at least part of what you say is true. Somebody sure as hell did kill a croc, and there's another one still here."

"This is the place he left us," Thornton said. "Carl was killed right there on the bank and dragged into the water by that other crocodile."

"That's not true!" Toby said. "This is where he killed the crocodile, but this is not where I left them."

The deputy said, "There's just one way to find out for sure about your friend." He raised the rifle and aimed it across the cove.

Toby sprang forward and grabbed the deputy's arm. He shouted, "No! Don't kill him! You cannot do this!

There will soon be none left!"

The deputy shoved Toby away. "Dammit, Tiger, stay out of this! I don't want to kill him, but there's no other way."

"Please don't do this," Toby pleaded. "This is not the place I left them. I swear it! Please don't kill him."

The deputy paid no heed to Toby's words as he aimed the rifle and fired. The magnum bullet knocked a hole as big as a grapefruit in the crocodile's head. It jumped forward and struggled for a moment, and then gushes of blood pumped from its head.

Toby's brown skin paled. He sank to his knees as the deputy went back to the airboat and returned with an axe and a large knife. Toby couldn't watch as the axe blade smashed downward again and again. He heard the thump of steel meeting flesh, but he kept his eyes cast downward.

Finally the deputy came back around the cove and said, "Wasn't nothing in there but gar fish, two coots and a possum." He turned to Thornton. "If that croc is supposed to have eaten your friend, where is he?"

"I don't know," Thornton said. "Maybe he's already digested him."

"Nope. I would have found bones and other evidence."

"Maybe that was the wrong croc."

"I don' see any others," the deputy said, putting down the axe. "Are you real sure your friend was killed?" he asked.

"I stood right over yonder and watched it."

"I mean did you actually see the crocodile eat him?"

"What do you want me to say?" Thornton said, becoming irritated. "I saw the crocodile jerk him into the water, and I saw him go under. If you mean did I run down there, stick my head under the water and watch it, the answer is hell no!"

"What did you do after your friend was jerked into the water?" the deputy asked.

"I tried to shoot, but my gun jammed. Then I guess I sort of blacked out for a while. I don't remember."

"For all you know, then, your friend could have got out of there and run off into the sawgrass, scared out of his wits."

"What the hell's this?" Thornton said angrily. "You tryin' to make me out a liar? I told you I stood right over yonder and watched him jerked into the water."

The deputy said nothing more. He walked around the cove and looked carefully, then he went into the brush and searched for a hundred yards around the island. When he returned, he said, "If this is the place Tiger left you, where is your gear and rifles?"

For a moment Thornton looked unsure of himself, and then he said cautiously, "I lost my rifle on the way out of the swamp. The gear was right over yonder. I guess somebody must have come along after I left here and stole it."

"Something else puzzles me," the deputy said. "How come that dead croc's stomach is cut open? Somebody started to skin out the hide but quit. Now who do you think could have done that?"

Thornton again spoke cautiously, "I don't know. Somebody must have come along after I left."

Toby was still squatting on the ground, listening. He

looked up and said, "This isn't the place I left them. The gear is not here. They must have come back here and tried to skin the crocodile after I left them on the other hammock."

Thornton glared at Toby and said, "Damn you, you stinkin' liar, I'm goin' to . . ."

"You're not going to do anything!" the deputy snapped. He turned to Toby. "Show me where it is you say you left them."

"You goin' to let that crazy Indian lead us on a wild goose chase all over this marsh?" Thornton asked. "I ain't got time to go on a sight-seein' tour."

The deputy ignored Thornton's remark and said to Toby, "You point the way, Tiger."

It took the fast airboat only a few minutes to reach the hammock. Toby walked straight from the shore to the small clearing and pointed to the two packs and rifles on the ground beside a palm trunk.

The deputy looked at the equipment and said to Thornton, "Is this your stuff?"

"I never saw it before."

After examining the packs, the deputy said, "If this isn't your stuff, why the hell is your name tag sewed onto this pack?"

Thornton stepped forward and looked at the pack. "Well, I guess it's mine. I just didn't recognize it at first. But I don't know how it got here. That Indian must have come back after I left that other place, stole the stuff and brought it here."

"If he stole it, why would he lead me straight to it now?" the deputy asked.

Thornton moved closer to the palm. He said, "Seems to me you're doin' nothin' but takin' up for that lyin' Indian. If you won't do nothin' about this, I will." He suddenly grabbed his rifle.

Before Thornton could throw the bolt, the deputy had a .44 pistol pointed directly into his face. The deputy said harshly, "Now you just put that rifle down, fellow! You try something like that again, I'll put cuffs on you!" Thornton leaned the rifle against the palm.

"I'm going to give you some good advice," the deputy said to Thornton. "Killing a crocodile or an alligator is a felony. For what you did you could spend a long time in jail plus pay a stiff fine. I could go over there and get the bullet from that croc's head, send it to the lab and match it to your rifle, and then you'd be in hot water up to your neck. Now as far as your friend is concerned, I'll get two more patrol boats out here this afternoon, and we'll search every foot of marsh for several miles around that island. If we find him, we'll bring him in. If we don't, he'll just have to be reported as a missing person. Either way, we'll send you a final report. As soon as we get back to Naples, I'd advise you to get into that camper and get the hell away from here as fast as you can, else I might change my mind and file charges against you. Do you understand what I'm saying?"

"I understand," Thornton said sullenly.

The deputy then turned to Toby and said, "As for you, I'm going to warn you to never again leave anyone out here alone no matter what the reason! Do you understand? After they killed the crocodile, you should have come straight back and reported them to the law."

Toby said, "I meant them no harm, but they did bad things. They killed without reason. And I was afraid that if I stayed with them, and they were caught with the hide, they would blame it on me."

"Well, you two get that stuff loaded into the boat," the deputy said, shaking his head. "This is the damnedest thing I've ever had to investigate. Let's get on out of here before I change my mind and arrest both of you."

As soon as they reached the village, Thornton and the deputy left in the patrol car. No further words were spoken among the three of them. Toby walked to Josie's chickee and sat on the bench.

Josie came from the pit, sat beside Toby and said, "Well, what happened out there?"

"The deputy found that what I said was truth. It is ended now."

"I'll bet you're glad of that."

"I am glad of nothing. The deputy killed another of the crocodiles and cut him open, and now only two are left. And he killed this one for nothing — the missing man was not there."

"You sure do take on about those crocodiles," Josie said. "You would think they are your kin."

"They are as all things I know and have known, even of the marsh itself," Toby said. "Soon it will all be ended, and there will be no more. The white men destroy all that they touch."

Josie got up and said, "Toby, why don't you go back to your camp and not wrestle today. Just spend the day taking it easy."

"No. I will stay here and wrestle. I need the money."

The two of them then walked through the village and to the pits.

FOURTEEN

T oby told Bentley the conclusion of the investigation by the deputy, but he didn't mention the affair to Lucy, not wanting her to even know that he had been taken into the marsh with Thornton and the deputy.

The next Monday morning he started his new job with anticipation. He had always liked to work with engines and anything mechanical, and he proved to be so good that Bentley let him do all of the buggy repairs in order to keep himself free to service regular garage and gasoline customers and help in the store.

The Everglades Hunting Club compound was located a mile down the Loop Road from Monroe Station, and Toby brought the swamp buggies to the garage one at a time. As soon as one was repaired, he returned it to the club storage shed and drove back with another. Bentley helped tow in the ones that wouldn't crank.

For the first week Toby worked from dawn to sunset each day, and he also worked Saturday and Sunday. His pay for the period came to eighty-five dollars. He didn't like to miss the weekend trip to his grandfather's hammock, and he determined that he wouldn't work again on weekend days; but it pleased him to know he would be able to pay the next rent on time and the bills and maybe save a little for the birth of the baby. When the time came, he would take Lucy to the medical clinic in Everglades City.

Toby stopped gigging frogs because of the continued drought, but he spent some time each night carving the wooden figures. He finished the crocodile he was making for the baby, and when he showed it to Lucy, she thought it to be the most perfect thing he had done. It was two feet long, and each minute detail of a crocodile's hide and body was as distinct as the real thing.

It was in the middle of his second week at Bentley's when Big Jim came into the garage one morning extremely worried. He said to Toby, "I just got back from the south swamp, and some damned fools have fired the woods. I was about a half-mile away when they saw me. They dropped their torches and high-tailed it out on a buggy. They were probably going to shoot wild hogs in front of the fire, but if we don't get it stopped before it spreads, that south wind will bring it right on up here. I've called the rangers and they should be out here soon."

Toby put down his tools and said, "What do you want me to do, Mr. Bentley? You want me to help with the fire or keep working on the buggies? I will do whatever you say."

Bentley thought for a moment, and then he said, "The woods are so dry that fire could move like it's running over spilled gasoline. I'll take the tractor and a disc and cut a fire lane around the meadow. You better get down to your camp and see about things there. If the fire comes that way, get out of there as quick as you can and bring Lucy back up here."

As Toby started for his truck, Bentley said, "Take one of those long lengths of hose from the shed and wet down your camp as best you can."

Toby got the hose and drove down the Loop Road. He could smell smoke although he couldn't see a smoke cloud or signs of fire. He churned up white dust as he pushed the pickup hurriedly along the rutted road.

When he reached the camp, Lucy was outside by the chickee. She ran to him immediately and said, "Toby, I have smelled smoke. Where is it coming from?"

"Someone has fired the woods south of Monroe Station, and I don't know if it will come this way or not."

Toby went to the faucet and hooked on the hose. When he turned the handle, a thin stream of water shot across the dry ground. He handed the hose to Lucy and said, "Keep the water running and wet everything in the camp. I'll go into the swamp and see what is happening."

Lucy was frightened just by the thought of fire. She said with concern, "Be careful, Toby. The woods are so dry you could be trapped out there."

"I'll be careful, and I will return soon. Keep the water running and wet everything."

Toby crossed the road in front of his camp and walked north. He did not come into this section of the swamp often, and he didn't know this land as well as the area to the south. The ground here was drier and more open than the dense swamp leading south to his airboat landing on Lost Creek.

He began to trot rapidly, and as he moved further

north, the smell of smoke became stronger. He had covered almost four miles before he saw the first sign of fire.

Even at the distance of a half-mile, Toby could feel the heat. Beads of sweat rolled down his chest, and his long hair was clinging to his neck. He watched as the top of a cabbage palm exploded like dynamite, sending a shower of sparks high into the air. The fire roared like the sound of the jet that night on the airport runway.

The wind was from the south, pushing the fire northward. Toby knew this presented no danger to his camp, but if the wind didn't change, Monroe Station would be in serious trouble. He watched for several minutes more as exploding trees made deep booming sounds, then he turned and ran back toward his camp.

Toby had a constant fear of such a fire breaking out in the Glades, rushing over the sawgrass and consuming the hammock of his grandfather. He knew that if this ever happened, the old man would be helpless to save himself. The sight of the hammock and the charred bodies of his mother and father came back into his mind vividly.

When he reached the camp, Lucy was spraying water onto the top of the chickee. He said to her, "The fire is moving northward. There is no danger here except for sparks drifting from the sky, but we must keep everything wet."

Toby got into the pickup and drove back toward Monroe Station to see if he could help Bentley. As he moved north the smoke became thicker until finally he couldn't see the road, then he turned the truck and went back to his camp.

Just at dusk the wind changed to the south, bringing with it clouds of choking smoke. Smoke poured into Toby's camp so thickly that Lucy went into the steaming bus and closed all of the windows. A dull glow lighted the sky to the north. As sparks drifted down into the camp, Toby put them out with the hose. His sweating body was black with soot as he moved about the clearing constantly, and it was long past midnight when he finally washed himself with the hose and went into the bus.

At daylight he was on his way to Bentley's place. The land just south of Monroe Station was charred black, and still smoldering. Smoke drifted on the air like fog, and soot covered the whiteness of the limestone road. As he drove nearer he dreaded what he might find, wondering if the building would be still standing or in ashes. He was greatly relieved when he came to the highway and found the old two-story structure still there.

Bentley was standing by the garage, gazing at the blackened pasture where the fire had finally stopped. He looked exhausted. When Toby came to him, Bentley said, "I guess we lucked out on this one. If the wind hadn't changed and backfired the fire, it would have jumped right over this place no matter what we did."

Toby followed Bentley into the store. Bentley went behind the counter and opened two beers, then they sat at a table as Bentley handed a beer to Toby and said, "You look like you could use one too. After last night, I need something cold instead of hot."

Bentley became silent for a moment, and then he said thoughtfully, "You know, Toby, sometimes I think it's just not worth it even trying to stay out here. You work your butt off to make a go of it, and then some damned fool comes along and fires the woods just for a few scrawny wild hogs that ain't worth a tinker's damn to nobody. Sometimes I feel like taking a torch, burning this place to the ground, saying to hell with it and moving on. It just ain't worth it."

Toby had never seen Bentley like this. He suddenly felt a closeness to him that he had never before felt toward any white man. He wanted to reach out and touch him, to establish a bond of understanding between the two of them. He also wanted to say something that would ease Bentley's depression, but he couldn't express himself as he wished. He only said, "I know, Mr. Bentley. Sometimes I have such thoughts myself."

Bentley took a deep drink of beer and said, "Your job went up in smoke too. Before we could stop it, the fire got into the hunting club grounds and burned the buggy storage sheds. Burned them right down to the ground, and there was nothing we could do. Now all of the buggies are gone. Seems like you've had nothing but hard knocks lately, and now this happens just so some bastard can take a shot at a pig running for its life."

The news shocked Toby, but he didn't want it to show. He said, "That's too bad, Mr. Bentley. I don't mind not having the work, but I'm sorry the fire did such a bad thing."

Bentley noticed the fear in Toby's eyes despite his attempt to hide it. He said, "I've been needing some help around the gas pumps and the garage. Suzie has a hard time when she has to handle the cafe and the grocery by herself. I couldn't pay much, maybe twenty bucks a week, but this would at least keep you in groceries till you find work. Could be your road job will be open again soon. You think about it, Toby, and let me know. You could start the first of next week."

Toby was already thinking before Bentley finished. He said, "I could also do carvings at night, and wrestle in the village on Sunday. And there are rabbits and turtles in the swamp, and we still have chickens. Maybe we can get by until something comes along. I will do this, Mr. Bentley. I will start the first of next week."

Bentley got up and said, "Let's go take a closer look at the damage."

Toby followed him outside, then they climbed onto the swamp buggy and headed south. Bentley drove rapidly over the smouldering ground, the buggy tires creating little black clouds of soot. They could see the charred bodies of rabbits, raccoons, armadillos, opossums, snakes and turtles. The deer, bear and wild hogs seemed to have outrun the fire to safety.

Bentley made a wide circle through the blackened swamp and then returned to the garage. He climbed off the buggy and said, "Well, I better find something to do and get with it before I change my mind and put a match to this place. It gets harder all the time just to survive, and sometimes it seems it just ain't worth the effort."

Toby went into the garage and put away his tools.

FIFTEEN

On Saturday morning, Toby left his camp earlier than usual. He had not visited his grandfather in more than two weeks and wanted to spend as much time with him this day as possible. He carried two bags of supplies he had purchased the night before.

He first turned the airboat west toward Allapattah Flats. When he reached the cove he took the cypress pole from the boat and made his way along the path.

Neither of the two remaining crocodiles were on the mud bank, but the dead ones were still there. Their flesh was rotted and torn into strips by vultures, and where the eyes had been there were now hollow sockets. Flies swarmed around the carcasses.

Toby knelt on the bank and searched the water for some sign of the others, then he looked at the carcasses and said, "I am sorry, old ones. I didn't want it to end this way for you. What happened to you is my fault. It was wrong for me to bring the white men here, and I will never do this again. I am sorry. But you shouldn't be there now where the others must lie."

He made his way around the end of the cove and approached the carcasses carefully. When he reached them he said, "I do not wish to come suddenly on your brothers in the bushes. Now is not the day for that."

The stink was overwhelming. Toby held his breath as he put the pole beneath one body and turned the crocodile over and over until he pushed it down a slight incline and into the water of the open bay. Then he rolled the other one in. "You will rest better in the water," he said. "It is not right for you to lie in the sun and be food for buzzards."

He then left the flats immediately and moved eastward. As he approached his grandfather's hammock he created his usual engine backfire and could see the old man come out of the palms and stand by the landing.

Toby embraced his grandfather and then took the packages from the boat. He said, "I am sorry to have been gone so long, Grandfather, but I worked on the weekend." The old man looked even more frail than during the last visit.

They walked up the path to the chickee and sat at the table. The old man said, "I saw great smoke in the north, and at night the sky was as red as the sunset. I was afraid you had been done harm."

"The fire didn't reach my camp," Toby said. "The south wind blew it north, and it did much damage around Monroe Station. All of the swamp buggies were burned at the hunting club, and many animals died in the woods."

"Fire is a bad thing," his grandfather said. "I have seen it leap over hammocks and race across the marsh like the wind, killing all in its way. I am glad it did you no harm."

Toby said, "I have brought many supplies, Grandfather. What would you like for your dinner?"

"You do not have it, but I would like deer. Many times lately I have hungered for the meat of the deer. That is what I liked most in my younger days. But I can hunt them no longer. I cannot go so far from the hammock."

Toby thought for a moment, and then he said, "If you want deer, you will have deer. I know a hammock where I've seen them lately. I will go kill one and then roast it over a fire. Is your shotgun in the chickee?"

"I did not mean for you to do that," the old man said quickly. "It was only foolish talk. I do not want you to go to such trouble for me."

"It will be no trouble at all. I will kill a buck and be back soon, and tonight you will have your fill of deer and eat until your stomach swells."

Toby went to the chickee and returned with an old double-barreled 12-gauge shotgun. He put a shell into each barrel, snapped the breech shut and said, "Gather some firewood while I'm gone, Grandfather. It will take a big fire to cook a whole deer."

The old man smiled. "I will have wood, and I will also make a spit for the roasting."

Toby pointed the airboat north toward a hammock a mile from the mouth of Lost Creek where he had seen deer the last time he passed that way. When he approached the area he stopped the engine and poled the airboat through the sawgrass, not wanting the noise of the engine to frighten away the deer if they were still there.

He moved to the shore slowly, and then he crept into a thick clump of palmetto. At this time of morning the deer would be lying on the ground, resting after a night of feeding, and they wouldn't be as alert as they were at first dawn.

Toby moved catlike from bush to bush, making his way toward the center of the hammock; then he moved to one side of a muscadine vine and stopped. Fifty feet to his left, a spike buck and two does were lying on a bed of bear grass. The buck's ears were turned back, and his head was tilted upward in an alert position.

When Toby cocked the hammers, the buck jumped to its feet. Both barrels fired at once. The two does bounded off into a thicket as the buck fell to the ground and kicked violently. Toby dropped the shotgun and ran forward, then he grabbed the buck's antlers and slit its throat with his hunting knife.

As soon as the kicking stopped, Toby cut open the buck's stomach and cleaned out the insides. He would wait until he reached the hammock before skinning out the meat. It was a small deer, weighing no more than sixty pounds on the hoof, but it would do. He retrieved the shotgun and carried the carcass back to the boat.

He gave the airboat full throttle, wanting to reach the hammock as quickly as possible. It would take several hours for the deer to cook, and he hoped his grandfather had already started the fire.

Toby was not aware of the airboat coming up swiftly behind him. It was a sleek craft much faster than his, and he was surprised when it shot in front of him and the driver signalled for him to stop. Painted across the side were the words, "Game and Fish Commission."

Toby eased back on the throttle and cut the engine, gliding his boat to a stop. The other boat turned and came along side of him. The driver wore a green uniform and had a .38 pistol strapped to his belt.

The game warden looked into Toby's boat and said, "I heard your shots back there. Got a deer, huh?"

"Yes," Toby said, looking down at the buck. "I killed it for my grandfather. He is very old, and he lives on a hammock alone. He has wanted deer meat badly and can no longer hunt for himself."

The warden said, "Well, I guess you know deer's out of season now. That's an illegal kill."

Toby felt a pang of fear. He had not even thought of the season. He said, "I know it's not the season, but I killed only for food. It is for my grandfather, and it is only a very small deer."

"Size doesn't matter. A deer's a deer. I'll have to place you under arrest."

Toby was startled. He studied the man for a moment, noticing that the warden was the same age as himself. He said, "In the past I killed one out of season for Grandfather and was stopped by a warden. When I told him why I shot the deer, he only warned me not to do this again and let me go. I haven't killed one out of season since then, but now Grandfather has hungered for deer."

The warden said, "If someone else turned his back on something like this, he shouldn't have. He could have gotten himself in trouble. We're out here to enforce the law. What's your name?"

"Toby Tiger. I live on the Loop Road, and I come out

here each week to bring supplies to Grandfather."

"Well, I'm afraid you're in for a bit of trouble. Indians have to obey the game laws just like everyone else, and if you wanted to kill a deer for your grandfather this time of year, you should have driven up to the reservation where the game laws don't apply. I'm sorry, but you're in possession of an illegal kill."

"What does this mean you will do?" Toby asked, now thoroughly frightened.

"You'll have to go to court. You could get a fine or a sentence or both, or the whole thing could be dropped. It depends on the judge. But we'll also have to take the shotgun and your airboat. That's the law."

It took a moment for Toby to digest the meaning of what the warden said. "You cannot do this!" he finally exclaimed. "It's my grandfather's gun, and I only borrowed it. Without the gun he cannot shoot the rabbit. He kills only for food. And without the airboat I cannot bring supplies each week."

"You should have thought about all that before you killed the deer," the warden replied. He noticed Toby's deep anguish and said, "Tell you what I'll do, though. I'll give you a break. I'm supposed to take you in right now and let you post bond until the hearing. I'll write you up and let you report on your own Monday morning in Everglades City."

"You cannot do this!" Toby repeated angrily. "It is only one small deer! It's for my grandfather, and he is very old! He doesn't have many days left!"

The warden eyed the shotgun lying in Toby's boat, and then his hand moved to the pistol. He had been a game warden for only six months and had just been transferred into the Everglades from Ocala. This was his first encounter with a Seminole. For a moment he wished he hadn't stopped the airboat, or that he had let Toby go when he explained about his grandfather; but he surmised that if he let him go now, it would appear that he had backed away from a problem. He said, "Listen, fellow, I'm just doing my job, and I'm also trying to do you a favor. I've given you a choice. I can take you in right now, or I can let you come in on your own. Which will it be?"

Toby realized there was no way out except to do as the warden instructed, that to resist would only make things worse. He said, "I will come next Monday to Everglades City. Can I go now and take the deer to my grandfather?"

"I'll have to keep the deer in case it's needed as evidence." The warden reached across and pulled the small buck into his boat. "Where do you dock this airboat?"

"On Lost Creek, near the entrance to the marsh."

"Well, just leave it there and we'll pick it up later today. I need the shotgun now."

Toby handed him the gun.

The warden seemed relieved that the shotgun was now in his boat. He wrote on a pad and handed a copy to Toby, then he said, "Report to the justice of the peace court in Everglades City at eight Monday morning, and I want to tell you something for your own good. If you're not there, you'll be in deep trouble. This could be a very simple thing, and for your sake I hope it is. But you must be in the court Monday morning. Do you understand?"

"Yes, I understand," Toby replied. "I will be there."

The warden cranked his engine, and as he moved away he shouted over the roar, "Be sure you leave the key in the airboat!"

As Toby watched the boat speed away to the east, he had a deep sickening feeling. It would have hurt less if the warden had only let him keep the deer. The warden was of his own generation, not of the time of the ruthless destroyers his grandfather spoke of, yet the warden didn't understand. It seemed to Toby that the warden had no sympathy for his grandfather and those before him who had lived on this land for centuries before the game laws were passed, laws created and designed only to keep other white men from destroying all that lived in nature. He knew it was not his people who raped the land, and the Seminoles had lived always by their own law of killing only for need. Over the years Toby had seen hundreds of deer die from the drought or drown in floods caused by the white men and their dikes and canals, but now only one deer killed for food presented him such trouble. He was angry at himself for being caught, and he also felt deep hatred for the warden and all others who enforced the white man's law. He couldn't believe the small buck to be worth the shotgun and his airboat, plus a fine and whatever else lay before him in Everglades City.

He finally started his boat and went back to the hammock, this time keeping the engine as quiet as possible when he approached. He found his grandfather still sitting at the table, sipping a cup of freshly brewed coffee.

To one side of the chickee there was a pile of wood with a spit of lancewood constructed over it.

Toby took a seat opposite his grandfather and said, "I have done a bad thing, Grandfather. I let the gun fall out of the boat, and I couldn't hunt the deer. I have lost your shotgun."

The old man showed no surprise or anger. He said, "It does not matter about the gun, Toby. I have not needed it lately. The gun was old and had no value."

Toby said, "In the packages I have corned beef and potatoes. Would you like for me to make a pot of stew?"

"If you wish," he replied. "I have not felt well lately, and I am not hungry. If you make the stew, I will try some later."

"You'll be hungry as soon as the heat of the day passes. It is only the heat. I will make the stew and leave it for you. And I am sorry about the deer and the shotgun."

When he finished cooking, Toby came back to the table. The old man was slumped forward, asleep. Toby touched his shoulder and said, "I must go now, Grandfather. There are things I must do."

He snapped awake. "I am glad you came, Toby. It is always good when you are here."

Toby walked back to the airboat with his arm around the old man's shoulder. Before he got into the boat he said, "Grandfather, I'll be back next Saturday and bring you a rifle from my camp. On the way I will kill a deer, then I'll spend the night and we will have a feast together."

"That would be good," his grandfather said, smiling.

"The wood will be waiting, and I have already made a spit for the roasting."

When he reached the camp, Toby went into the bus, opened a beer and came back out to the chickee. Lucy was sitting by the grill. She said, "I didn't expect you back so soon. How is your grandfather?"

"I don't think he is well. He fell asleep at the table while I was cooking his stew, and he wouldn't eat. I have never seen him do this. Always before he has had an appetite. I have heard that when old Seminole men know they are dying, they wander off into the swamp alone, searching for the place of their birth. It wouldn't surprise me to go out there soon and find him gone."

"I wish he would come and live here," Lucy said. "He would be good company for me, and I would see that he gets proper food."

Toby took another drink of beer, not wanting to speak of what happened but knowing he must. He said, "Lucy, I'm in some trouble and you will have to know of it."

She looked up quickly, and then she came over and sat at the table. "What is it?"

He spoke hesitantly, "Grandfather said that he has hungered lately for venison. I took his shotgun, went to a hammock and killed a small deer. On the way back I was stopped by a warden, and he placed me under arrest. He also took grandfather's gun and will take my airboat later today. I have to be in court next Monday morning in Everglades City."

Lucy's face flushed with fear. She said, "What does

this mean? What will they do to you?"

"I do not know. The warden said I could get a fine or a jail sentence or both, or even nothing. It is up to the judge. But I'm sure they won't put me in jail for killing one deer. I will tell the judge why I did it and he will probably let me go with a warning."

"Why don't you see Mr. Bentley about this? He would go with you and help."

Toby shook his head in disapproval and said, "No, I'll not do that. Mr. Bentley has done enough for me already. I'll not bother him with this."

"He will help if you ask," Lucy insisted.

Toby wanted to minimize his trouble to Lucy and ease her concern. He said, "I am not worried about what will happen in the court Monday. We have more than enough money in the coffee can to pay the fine if that is what they do to me. What bothers me most is the airboat. I need it as much as the pickup. Maybe I can find another airboat with a bad engine and rebuild it myself as I did before. When I get back Monday I'll go down to the airboat place on the Trail and see what they have."

"Will you at least tell Mr. Bentley about this?" Lucy asked.

"Yes. I'll stop by there Monday morning and tell him, but there's no need for you to worry. The fine will not be so much for one deer, and I can soon save money again for the baby."

SIXTEEN

Dawn was breaking as Toby arrived at Monroe Station Monday morning. The garage was locked, so he went into the store. Several men were seated at tables, eating breakfast. Suzie Bentley was behind the cafe counter, but Big Jim wasn't there.

Toby sat on a stool and said, "Where can I find Mr. Bentley?"

Suzie turned away from a skillet of eggs and said, "He's not here right now, Toby. He went down to the south swamp just a few minutes ago, but he should be back in an hour. You need the garage key?"

"No, I don't need the key. When he gets back, please tell Mr. Bentley I can't work this morning. I have a trip to make and I'll be back as soon as I can."

"Yeah, I'll tell him, Toby. You want something to eat or some coffee?"

"Thanks, but I've already eaten," Toby replied. "I have to go now. Just tell Mr. Bentley I'll be back as soon as I can."

As Toby drove west he thought of the many times he had traveled this section of highway at dawn on his way to the road maintenance headquarters north of Copeland. For a long time he had been angry about the loss of his job, but now he was glad he no longer had to drive so far each day to and from work. And he enjoyed working at Bentley's much more than chopping bushes, cutting grass and replacing drainage culverts.

He also tried to convince himself that what he soon faced in Everglades City would be minor and of no real consequence. Even if the fine took all of his savings for the rent and for the baby, he could replace some of it with his work at Bentley's and by carving cypress figures at night. Somehow, too, he would replace the airboat. Yet all of his self-assurances couldn't erase a deep undercurrent of fear.

When he reached the Highway 29 junction he turned south to drive the final three miles into Everglades City. Once before he had been to this same courtroom with Josie Billie when Josie had to appear before the judge and was fined thirty-five dollars for driving the Mustang too fast along the Trail.

The streets of the town were deserted as the dust-covered pickup ambled around a corner and parked in front of a two-story stucco building that served as town hall and courthouse. Paint on the windows and doors was flaked in strips, and the old building seemed to have settled into the muck earth and tilted to the left.

Toby was thirty minutes early, so he sat in the pickup and watched as an occasional car rattled along the street. In the distance he could hear the shrill cry of sea gulls as they swarmed over the waterfront, searching for food. When finally several people entered the building, he got out of the truck.

There was no one in the entrance foyer, but an arrow pointed upward to the Justice of the Peace Court. Toby climbed the wooden stairs to the second floor and entered a small room lined with benches. A deputy in uniform sat in a chair beside a closed door leading into an adjoining room. Toby sat on one of the benches and waited.

The deputy leafed through a file of papers, and shortly after eight o'clock he stood up and said, "Toby Tiger."

Toby was startled by the sound of his name coming from the stranger. He said apprehensively, "I am Toby Tiger."

The deputy opened the inner door and said, "In here."

The small room contained a large desk with several wooden chairs in front. On the right corner of the desk there was a small American flag, and on the left a state flag. Behind the desk, the wall was decorated with a framed copy of the Bill of Rights, a membership certificate in the Chamber of Commerce, a Kiwanis plaque, and a calendar from a sporting goods store in Naples. Pictured on the calendar was a scene of a man pointing a shotgun at a flight of ducks.

Toby sat in the room alone for several minutes, and then the judge entered from another door on the left. He was a man in his middle forties with thick hair bleached sun-yellow. His face looked as if he spent much time each day outdoors, and his walk was brisk as he came to the chair behind the desk and sat down.

The judge paid no heed to Toby as he examined papers on the desk, then finally he looked up and said,

"Your name, please."

"Toby Tiger."

The judge then said, "Do you know the nature of this court?"

"I am not sure," Toby replied.

"This is a justice court. We don't have trials by jury here. If you plead guilty, I will hear your case now and decide on the outcome. If you wish, you can request a jury trial in circuit court. In this event, you would then hire an attorney and your case would be heard in Naples. Do you understand?"

"Yes, I understand," Toby replied.

The judge asked, "What is your wish in this matter?"

Toby had not known he would have a choice, and he was not prepared for such a decision. He said, "I have done nothing wrong. What would be the cost of the attorney?"

The judge looked at Toby quizzically. "I can't tell you that. It depends on who you hire. There's no set fee but I'm sure it would run at least a thousand dollars to go into circuit."

"I cannot pay so much," Toby said, surprised by the figure.

The judge remained silent for a moment as he studied a piece of paper, then he looked again at Toby and said, "You are charged with deer poaching. It says here that Warden Simms apprehended you with an illegal deer in your airboat. Is this true?"

"Yes, this is true. He stopped me in the Glades as I was on my way to my grandfather's hammock with the deer."

"If this is true, and you say it is true, you would surely
be found guilty in a circuit court. You would fare better
here. Do you want me to hear the case or not?"

Toby was confused. He wished now he had done as
Lucy insisted and brought Bentley with him. He
responded, "If I would be found guilty in the court in
Naples, there is no need to go there. And I don't have
money for an attorney."

The judge looked annoyed as he said impatiently,
"We have a full docket this morning and I can't spend all
day on one case. You will have to give me a definite
answer."

"We will finish it here," Toby said.

"Good. Now tell me what you have to say about this
case."

"I have done nothing wrong."

For a moment the judge looked as Toby remembered
the white teacher looking at him each day in the school
classroom. He said, "Just tell me what happened. Can
you do something as simple as that?"

"Yes." Toby turned his eyes directly to the judge as he
spoke. "My grandfather is very old, and he lives on a
hammock alone. He is not well, and he can no longer
hunt for himself. Each week I carry supplies to him, as
much as I can afford. When I went to the hammock that
morning, Grandfather said he had hungered lately for
deer. I took his shotgun and went to another hammock
where I killed a small buck. I was on my way back to
Grandfather's hammock to cook the deer when the
warden stopped me."

"I understand your concern for your grandfather," the

judge said, "but didn't you know you were killing the deer out of season?"

"I knew it was not the season, but I didn't think of it at the time. I killed the deer only for food for my grandfather, and it was a very small deer."

"What you intended to do with the buck is not at issue," the judge said. "When you killed the deer out of season you knowingly broke the law. That is the only thing at issue."

"But it was only for food," Toby stressed. "I didn't kill without reason."

"There is no 'reason' when it comes to rules of law," the judge said. "You have either broken the law or you haven't, and in this case, you have clearly broken the law. When a case comes before this court I must act according to law, and the law applies to all people the same. This is what we call equal justice before the law. When a person breaks the law for any reason, he must be prepared to pay the penalty. And we must protect our wildlife or there will soon be no more. There is little enough left now for everyone to hunt without someone killing out of season. It is such acts as you committed that will soon make our wildlife vanish. Do you understand what I am saying?"

Toby did not understand. He repeated, "I have done nothing wrong. I killed only for food for my grandfather. He is very old, and he has but a few days left. He has lived all of his days in the marsh, but now he is too old to hunt for himself."

The judge leaned back in the chair and looked toward the entrance door. He said, "In this case I can do nothing but find you guilty as charged. You have admitted this yourself. Your sentence will be a five-hundred-dollar fine and thirty days in jail. Because of the circumstances behind your breaking the law, I will suspend the thirty days and place you on one year's probation. You also owe twenty dollars for cost of court, and you can pay the fine and the court cost to the clerk downstairs."

Toby didn't move. For the first time that morning, he felt deep fear. He said, "I don't have five hundred dollars."

"Is there someone who can pay it for you?"

"I know no one who can pay so much."

"If you cannot pay the fine, you will have to serve the time in jail. A deputy will transport you to the jail in Immokalee."

Toby stood up, took a roll of bills from his pocket and said, "I have seventy-five dollars. I can pay this now and some each Saturday." He put the bills on the desk.

The judge picked up the money and handed it back to Toby. "All fines have to be paid in full. If you don't have all of the money, and you can't get someone to put up the rest, then you must serve the time. The deputy will escort you to Immokalee."

Anger suddenly flushed through Toby. He shouted, "No! I will not do this! I must take supplies to my grandfather each week, and my wife is with child!"

"One more outburst like that and you'll get an extra thirty days for contempt of court!" the judge said sternly. "This case is ended! Do you understand that?"

"And what of my wife, Lucy?" Toby asked, his voice now reflecting both defeat and concern. "Will someone tell her that I will be gone for a while?"

"Where do you live?" the judge asked.

"On the Loop Road, about ten miles from Monroe Station."

"Do you live in chickees?"

"We live in a bus, but there is a chickee behind it. I rent the camp from a man in Miami. It will be easy to find."

The judge said, "I will have a deputy go by there and tell her the next time one is down that way." He pushed a button on the desk and the entrance door opened. A deputy stepped inside, and the judge said to him, "The prisoner is to be escorted to the jail in Immokalee in his own vehicle."

"Yes, sir, judge," the deputy said. "I'll get someone here right away."

Toby was not aware of the road or the traffic or the scenery or the deputy sitting beside him as he drove north to Immokalee. Even the details of the brief trial were but an incomprehensible blur in his mind. He was remembering the days when he was young and his father came into the camp with a deer he had killed for food for the family, and he was remembering tales told by his grandfather of white men coming into the marsh to slaughter the alligator for its hide and the egret for its plumes, white men killing deer and bear by the hundreds and selling the meat for two cents a pound, sometimes leaving the bodies on the ground to rot when there were too many to carry; but now he must leave Lucy and his grandfather for killing one deer for food.

He also thought of the many skeletons he had found in the marsh because the white men drained the land with canals, diked it and turned the water away, destroying food for the deer and other animals; and then his mind drifted to that morning when he watched helplessly as the white man pumped bullets into the crocodile's brain, shattering the life from it for no reason, and they didn't even take the man's rifle from him. It was impossible for him to put all of the pieces together and make sense or reason or justice from what the judge had done to him. He felt only deep bitterness.

He drove by instinct into the city limits and to the bright modern building housing the county's branch courthouse and jail. The deputy escorted him inside to a room where he was photographed and fingerprinted. His personal belongings were put into a brown envelope, and then he was led down a white corridor lined on both sides with cells.

SEVENTEEN

Lucy moved the wooden spoon absently, unaware that she had stirred the pot continuously for more than an hour. It contained a small portion of chicken stew, but it was enough for one person. For most meals she ate only a piece of cold chicken or a tomato. In the intense heat it seemed pointless to her to sit by the grill and cook hot meals only for herself.

During the day she watered the garden and cleaned the bus and spent long hours at the sewing machine, mending and then re-mending Toby's clothes, or making something for the baby. Until the time she ran out of thread and cloth, she had made enough things for the birth of twins. She managed to keep busy during the days, but the nights were long and lonely and filled with sleepless hours.

A deputy sheriff did not come by and tell her the results of the trial until three days after Toby was jailed, and she was frantic with fear and anxiety when the green patrol car finally turned into the camp. Afterwards, she sat at the table beside the chickee, crying constantly for the better part of an afternoon. She gradually accepted the fact that Toby wouldn't be with her for a month.

She then went into the bus and examined the shelves and cabinets. There was a fair supply of staples such as flour, cornmeal and salt, and also a few cans of beans. She would have to do without milk, but there were chickens in the clearing, and she could shoot the rifle well enough to kill rabbits in the swamp. And there were vegetables in the garden. There would be enough to survive on for a month until he returned.

Many times during the coming days she thought of asking Bentley to take her to the home of her parents on the reservation so she could pass the time there. But each time she started to stand by the road and catch a ride to Monroe Station, she realized it was a long way to the reservation, and as Toby had said, this was not Bentley's problem. She didn't want to cause him bother.

Toby had been away for two weeks on the morning Lucy got out of bed feeling ill. Her head spun, and she steadied herself against a shelf. She thought immediately of morning sickness and thought it would soon pass.

When the dizziness did not stop, Lucy went to the refrigerator and poured herself a glass of cold water. Even early in the morning, the inside of the bus was like a furnace. Sweat poured from her forehead as she sat at the table and sipped the water.

She finally got up to go outside for fresh air, but when she approached the door, she again had to steady herself against a cabinet.

For several minutes she stood still, thinking perhaps it would be better to go back and lie on the bed. Sweat dripped into her eyes, hazing her sight, then she moved instinctively toward the outside. Her foot caught on a thin ledge beneath the door, causing her to pitch forward and fall headlong to the ground.

She immediately tried to push herself up. Her arms strained, but her swollen body would not move. Then the dizziness became worse. When she looked upward, the tops of cypress trees resembled vague, ghostly flights of egrets. She then looked across the clearing, her eyes searching for some sight of Toby coming along the path from the swamp.

When she realized Toby would not come, she pictured him leaving the clearing at night with his gig, dressed in the cut-off jeans she had patched so often, his brown body glistening with shadows from the fire; and she could see him running with the wind in the airboat, moving with reckless abandon across vast stretches of marsh, visiting the crocodiles he spoke of so often, carrying food to his grandfather, sitting by the fire at night carving blocks of cypress into living things; remembering his defiance of her father . . . *God is everything . . . the water the trees the animals the land . . . they are killing God . . . His face in the swamp . . . shot God through the head for a few fish . . .*; thinking of his love of the old ways, insisting she wear the traditional ankle-length dress for their wedding in her father's church on the reservation, coming to Toby's camp, hesitant, walking hand in hand past lush beds of thick ferns in the swamp, then beneath a cypress tree, and again by Lost Creek with the moon playing its special magic, wondering about him now, seeing him in all ways except in the jail cell in Immokalee.

All of these thoughts suddenly merged into a mass of darkness. Her arms jerked as a sharp pain raced through her stomach. She tried once again to push herself up, but it was impossible. She whispered feebly, "Toby . . ." And then she lay still.

EIGHTEEN

~~~~~~

Toby's first few days in the cell were almost unbearable. He paced back and forth constantly, walking from wall to bars and back again, trying desperately to think of some way to get himself out of this impossible situation. The stale air choked his lungs, and he ached to be outside when the sun first reddened the sky and when the magical twilight hour came. He thought much of Lucy, wondering if she had enough to eat, hoping that Bentley or someone would visit her and see to her needs. He also worried about his grandfather and hoped that his supplies would last until he could get out of the cell and visit the hammock once again. Each day passed slowly and miserably as one week merged into another.

Toby was sitting on the bunk, looking without interest through a magazine, when he heard the key click in the cell lock. At first he thought it was his breakfast being served, but the man carried no tray. He motioned for Toby to come outside.

Toby hesitated, and then the guard said, "You can get your things in the office, Tiger. Your fine's been paid."

Realization came slow. "Who has done this?" Toby

asked.

"I don't know," the guard replied. "I was just told to let you out."

Toby followed the guard down the corridor and into a small office. Another man handed him the brown envelope containing his money and personal things. He pointed toward another door and said, "That way."

As soon as he entered the lobby he heard the word spoken loudly, "Toby!" It was Lucy's father. He came to Toby quickly and said, "We didn't know of this, Toby. If we had, you wouldn't be here. You should have sent word somehow."

"I didn't know of a way to do this," Toby said. "But who paid the fine? It was so much money."

"I paid half, and Mr. Bentley half. I wanted to pay it all myself, and he also wanted to send all of it. Then he insisted he at least pay half. Mr. Bentley didn't know of this until two days ago. When you didn't show up for work, he thought you had gone off to stay with your grandfather. He said had he known in the beginning, you would never have come to this jail."

"I will repay both of you," Toby said. "It was so much money."

"There is time later to think of that, and there's no hurry." Lucy's father then touched Toby's shoulder and said, "Let's sit over here for a moment, Toby."

They walked to a line of chairs against the lobby wall. Toby was anxious to get out of the building and return to his camp, but he knew that Lucy's father had something he wished to say, and Toby appreciated what he had done. He would listen patiently.

The reverend seemed hesitant, not wanting to speak further, and for a moment he just looked at Toby. Then he put his hand on Toby's arm and said, "It is about Lucy."

Toby said immediately, "Has something happened to her?"

"She will be fine," the reverend said quickly. "She is at our house on the reservation."

"Tell me what has happened!" Toby urged.

Lucy's father spoke slowly. "She got up one morning feeling sick, and then she fell from the bus. It was Mr. Bentley who found her. He had gone to the camp to inquire of you. Lucy had dragged herself to the chickee, and that is where the baby came."

"The baby came?" Toby questioned, his voice trembling with fear of what he would hear next.

"Yes, beneath the chickee. It was a boy. But he died, Toby. It was not his time, and he died before anything could be done for him. I am sorry. I hated to tell you of this."

Toby was silent with shock, feeling as if lead had been poured into his veins. "When did this happen?" he finally asked.

"Two days ago. I would have come here yesterday, but I broke the axle on my truck just as I left the reservation and had to fix it."

"And what of the baby?" Toby asked. "What was done with my son?"

"Mr. Bentley brought Lucy and the baby to the reservation. I buried him there in the cemetery beside the church."

Toby jumped up and said, "I will go there now!"

"Leave the truck and ride with me," Lucy's father said. "You shouldn't be driving now. We can return for your truck at another time."

Toby said nothing more as he rushed from the building and to his pickup. When he turned onto the road leading to the reservation, he pushed the old truck's accelerator to the floor, not caring if he broke the speed limit or if he smashed into a stray cow that wandered into his way. The hot asphalt zipped by in a blur, and soon he raced past the reservation entrance and skidded the truck to a stop in the clearing beside the church.

Dust drifted onto the porch as he ran up the steps and into the house. Lucy was in the parlor with her mother. She came to him quickly and cried, "Toby . . . Toby . . ."

As he held her in his arms he could feel fear draining from her as her frail body trembled against him. He said to her, "I'm sorry, Lucy. This would not have happened if I had been at the camp, and there is no reason for this."

Lucy looked at the anger and the hostility in his eyes, and then she said, "It was an accident, Toby. Don't blame yourself or anyone. It was only an accident. And I am so sorry about the baby."

"Where is the grave?" Toby asked.

"Beside the church, just inside the front gate. Pappa gave him a Christian burial."

"I will dig him up, and then he will lie on the hammock with my mother and my father and my grandmother!"

Lucy stepped back, shocked and horrified by what

he said. She said, "Do not do this thing, Toby! Wait until Pappa gets here and speak with him first."

"I will dig him up!" Toby repeated. "He is my son and the grandson of my father, and he will lie with the others!"

Lucy's face whitened. She said, "Toby, please listen to me! Do not do this."

Before she could finish he raced from the room and to a shed behind the house. He grasped the shovel firmly as he ran to the side of the church and into the small cemetery. After removing a vase of flowers from the fresh grave, he struck the ground savagely. Dirt flew aside wildly as he started unearthing the coffin.

Just then Lucy's father ran into the cemetery. He pleaded, "Do not do this, Toby! You're on sacred ground! It is God's will the baby is dead, and now he is with the Lord!"

Toby stopped for a moment and said angrily, "It is not God's will! It is the will of the devil! It is the will of the white men who took me from Lucy!"

Lucy's father shook his head in anguish as Toby struck the ground again and again. Then Toby threw the shovel aside and snatched the small coffin from the grave. He took it in his arms, rushed back to the house and placed it in the back of the truck.

Lucy came outside. Toby turned to her and said, "We will go now."

Her eyes were moist as she said, "I cannot come with you, Toby. I am not well enough for the trip. I must stay here for a few days, and then Pappa will bring me home."

As Toby climbed into the cab, Lucy started to run

to him and try to reason with him again. Her father grabbed her arm and said, "No, Lucy! Now is not the time to interfere. He would not hear you. Let him go."

She watched as the pickup sped away from the house and disappeared down the road, then her father steadied her as she almost toppled forward into the dust.

NINETEEN

~~~~~~~~~~~~~~~~~~~~~~~~~~~~~~~~~~~

I t was noon when Toby reached the camp. He went into the bus and put on the warrior clothes and the medicine bag, then he opened a cabinet and took out the carved crocodile he had made for the baby. He put the wood against his knee and snapped it in half, carrying it with him out to the coffin.

He walked swiftly through the swamp, not seeing the birds or the barking squirrels or the rabbits that scurried out of his way. When he reached Lost Creek he went automatically to the airboat landing, but the boat was not there. Then he pushed the cypress dugout canoe into the water and placed the small coffin and the broken carving in the bow. He picked up the slender cypress pole and moved away silently down the creek.

When he reached the beginning of the marsh he paused for a moment, looking down at the coffin and the broken crocodile. He breathed deeply, as if trying to draw the marsh itself into his body, and then he moved the canoe swiftly into the sawgrass.

Night had come when Toby returned to the deserted camp. He went into the bus and flicked on the light switch. When nothing happened and the bus remained in darkness, he realized he had not paid the electric bill and the power had been cut off. This also meant that the well pump wouldn't work, and there would be no water in the camp. He lit a kerosene lamp and placed it on the table, then he opened the refrigerator for a beer, but there was none. He then went outside to the truck and drove away toward Monroe Station.

Several tables in the cafe were filled with people when Toby entered. He walked through the room and into the grocery section, finding Bentley behind the counter. Bentley noticed Toby's strange clothes and the turban but made no comment. He waited, and finally Toby said, "I thank you for what you have done, Mr. Bentley."

Bentley said, "It's O.K., Toby. But why didn't you let me know about this when it happened? If I'd known, you would never have gone to Immokalee."

"I didn't want to bother you with it," Toby said. He handed Bentley a roll of bills. "I have seventy-five dollars here, and I'll work out the rest as soon as I can."

Bentley refused the money. He handed it back and said, "Keep it, Toby. You might need it now for something else. We'll square up later."

"It is yours if you wish," Toby said.

"No," Bentley said again. "We'll square up later."

"The electricity has been cut off at my camp," Toby said. "Do you know how much it is that I owe?"

Bentley looked in a card file on a shelf, then he said, "It's twenty-five dollars. I didn't realize it was past due."

Toby counted out the money and handed it to

Bentley, and then Bentley said, "I'll see to it that the power is turned on again first thing in the morning."

Toby handed another bill to Bentley and said, "I would like two cartons of beer."

Bentley took the beer from a cooler, put it into a paper bag and handed it and the change to Toby. He said, "I'm sorry about Lucy and the baby. Real sorry. That was a bad thing to happen."

"He is fine now. I took him this afternoon to the hammock of my mother and my father and my grandmother. He is with the others now, and he is at peace."

Bentley said, "Toby, take a few days to yourself before you come back to work."

Toby picked up the package. "I may do this. And I thank you again for what you have done for me and for Lucy."

All of the people in the cafe had noticed Toby when he had entered and had watched him curiously. As he passed back through the room, one man sitting alone laughed and said loudly, "What kind of an outfit is that you got on, chief? I didn't know they had a cowboy and Indian circus going on out here in the swamp."

Toby turned to the man. He whipped the knife from its sheath and slammed it into the top of the table, and then he said bitterly, "Shut your mouth, you goddam chicken snake! Or I will slit you open like a fish!"

The man looked at the intense anger in Toby's face and at the long knife imbedded in the wood. He moved his chair backwards as he said, "I'm sorry, fellow. I didn't mean anything. I was just trying to be funny."

Toby jerked out the knife and tightened his grip on

the handle as he moved the blade towards the man's throat. Steel touched flesh before he hesitated and said, "What is it that's so funny, chicken snake?" Then he rammed the knife back into the sheath and left hurriedly.

For a moment no one in the cafe seemed to breathe, and even the noisy air conditioner lost its sound. The man finally turned to Bentley and said, "What's the matter with that fool Indian? Is he crazy?"

Bentley looked toward the door and then back to the table. He said, "No, he's not crazy. I guess he's just had about all he can cut. You're lucky he didn't slice you up like a watermelon. You better learn when to keep your mouth shut."

The man took a deep drink of beer, wiped his mouth and said again, "I was just trying to be funny, that's all. I didn't mean anything by it."

TWENTY

For two days Toby stayed in the camp alone. He would sit at the table for a time and carve cypress blocks, then he would get up and pace back and forth across the clearing. Several times he walked through the swamp to the empty airboat landing on Lost Creek, poled the old dugout canoe to the edge of the marsh and stared intensely toward a distant hammock. He also wore the medicine bag constantly, sometimes talking to it as if speaking to Lucy or his grandfather.

On the third morning he left the camp early and drove past the Osceola Village to the Gator Airboat Sales. When he reached the place he parked in front of a small office and walked through the sales lot. Several airboats were on trailers, and others rested on the bank of a creek leading into the marsh.

As Toby looked carefully at the boats, a man came from the office and joined him. Toby said, "Hello, Mr. Thompson."

"Hi, Toby," the man replied. "What can I do for you?"

"I need a boat."

Thompson said, "A warden told me what happened with the deer. I didn't know it was you, though, until they brought your boat in here for storage. What'd they do to you?"

Toby was surprised that Thompson knew, and also surprised that his boat was here. He said, "I went to court in Everglades City. The fine was five hundred dollars or thirty days in jail, and I didn't have the money."

Thompson whistled. "Five hundred bucks or thirty days for one deer! You must have caught Judge Lambert. He's a real bastard. Last year him and three other guys got caught shooting doves on a baited field out from Clewiston. Got off scot-free. He fined a friend of mine a hundred bucks for having one bass over the limit. Too bad you didn't have a faster boat, Toby. You could have outrun the warden."

Toby said, "Do you have another boat with a bad engine like I bought before?"

"Sure don't. I only have a few used boats in stock. You want to see what I have?"

"Yes. I must have a boat."

Toby followed Thompson to the bank of the creek, then Thompson pointed and said, "These three."

Toby glanced briefly at the boats and said, "Which is the cheapest?"

"Well, they're all in top shape. The one on the end I could let go for twelve hundred."

The figure was impossible to Toby, but he knew he must have a boat even if it took him the rest of his life to pay for it. He said, "I have forty dollars to pay down, and the rest I'll pay each Saturday."

The man shook his head. "Can't do that, Toby. We have to have a third down on used boats. That would run you four hundred."

"I could pay more each Saturday."

"Just no way. But why don't you buy your old boat back? They'll sell it at auction, and boats don't bring much of nothing that way."

Toby had not thought of this. He asked anxiously, "When will they sell it?"

"Probably three or four weeks. Whenever they get around to it."

"I can't wait that long," Toby said, disappointed. He looked down the bank at his boat. "I will have to do something sooner."

As Toby walked back to his truck, Thompson called after him, "You get some more money, Toby, come back and see me. That boat's in top shape. It can outrun any of those patrol boats."

Toby drove back west and stopped when he reached Osceola Village. As he walked through the souvenir store, he wished he had brought the few finished carvings with him. He met Josie coming from the pits, and they went to the chickee together.

Josie poured two mugs of coffee and said, "I heard what happened. I was up by your camp one day and Lucy told me. That's a hell of a note, so much trouble over one deer. Lucy was very worried. How is she?"

"She's at the reservation."

"Why is she there?" Josie asked.

"You don't know?"

"I know nothing more than I've said. She seemed fine except that she was concerned for you. Why did she go to the reservation?"

Toby said, "She fell from the bus one morning while I was gone. The baby came, and it died. She is spending a few days with her mother and father before she returns to the camp."

Josie was surprised. Sympathy crossed his face as he said, "I didn't know, Toby. I'm sorry. You seem to have much bad luck lately."

Toby didn't want to discuss it further. He said, "I tried to buy a used airboat, but the cheapest was twelve hundred. I couldn't make the down payment and they wouldn't take less. I haven't taken supplies to Grandfather since they let me out of jail, and I must have a boat."

"I can let you have fifty dollars," Josie said.

Toby said, "I appreciate the offer, but that wouldn't be near enough. They want four hundred down and I have only forty. But there is a way. My boat is stored at Gator Sales. Mr. Thompson says it will be sold at auction in a few weeks, and that it will bring little. I might have enough money by then to buy it back, but I can't wait that long. I will take it back."

"You mean steal it?" Josie asked.

"How can I steal what is mine? They shouldn't have taken it from me in the first place. I did nothing wrong. I will take only what is mine."

"Well, if you get caught, you know what will happen," Josie cautioned. "That is as bad as stealing a car."

"I don't give a damn about that!" Toby said harshly. "If someone comes on me, I will stick a knife in them."

Josie eyed Toby curiously, and then he said, "In that case, I hope you're not caught. Then you would be in more trouble than you've ever known."

Toby said, "If you'll drive me down there tonight, I will wire the ignition and go across the marsh in the darkness. I can hide the boat on Lost Creek."

"Is that all you want me to do, take you down there?"

"Yes."

Josie sighed. "I will do that, Toby, but nothing more. You've almost gotten me into jail before. It would seem that you like it in Immokalee."

"No one will see," Toby insisted. "And I must have a boat now."

"I will pick you up at your camp late this afternoon. But if you'll not do this thing, I will pass the hat around the village and try to raise the down payment."

Toby said again, "I will only take what is mine."

It was an hour after dark when Josie let Toby out of the Mustang just west of Gator Sales. Josie said, "Be careful, Toby. Don't let anyone see you or you'll be in great trouble, much more than the deer. And if you do get caught, don't do something foolish. The airboat is not worth it."

Toby made no response. He put on the medicine bag and strapped the long warrior knife to his side, then he took a pair of wire cutters from the car and walked slowly along the edge of the highway. When he reached the creek he went down the bank and directly to his boat. The sales office was bathed with light from several floodlights, but the place was deserted.

Toby's boat was chained and locked to a post. He cut the chain with the wire cutters and pushed the boat backward into the water, then he got in and poled it down the creek.

Two miles out into the marsh he stopped and looked back at the glow of the floodlights. Ahead of him lay vast stretches of darkness. He then wired the ignition, started the engine and moved away slowly.

From this point to Lost Creek was more than twenty-five miles, and he would have to run at less than half speed and be very careful. Once when running the boat on the marsh at night he had hit a stump, thrown himself out and damaged the boat. This night he wanted no injury to himself or to the boat.

There was no moon, and the hammocks were ghostly forms drifting on a sea of darkness. Several times he heard loud thumps beneath the airboat as he ran over either logs or alligators. He drove the boat by instinct, searching constantly for sights of things familiar. When finally he came to a solid line of pond cypress, he knew he had reached the edge of the swamp. From here he veered west, and soon afterwards he found the mouth of Lost Creek.

When he reached his landing he took the airboat farther up the creek than usual, then he pulled it onto the bank and covered it with bushes and palmetto fronds.

He had to feel his way slowly through the black swamp, and when he approached the camp, the clearing was bathed with flickering light from a fire beneath the chickee. This startled him, and he moved forward cautiously. Then he saw that Lucy was there. She was sitting by the grill, cooking something in the pot.

She jumped up when he came from the shadows. "I have wondered where you were," she said, coming to him. "Since your truck is here I thought you would be in the swamp. Pappa brought me late this afternoon."

He took her in his arms and said, "I am glad you are here. I have been lonely without you."

She was pleased that he missed her. "Have you eaten yet?" she asked. "I've been keeping a supper hot for you."

"No, I have not eaten, and I'm starved."

Toby ate ravenously, and then they talked. He said, "I have the airboat back. I will go tomorrow and take supplies to Grandfather."

"How did this happen?" she asked.

"It was stored at the airboat sales place on the Trail. I took it from there."

"You took it?" Lucy questioned. "They didn't give it back to you when the fine was paid?"

"No, I took it. I've just brought it across the marsh to Lost Creek."

Worry crossed Lucy's face. She said, "Toby, do you mean you have stolen the boat?"

"How can I steal what is mine? I took back only what belongs to me. They have no right to my boat."

"Will this not mean great trouble?"

"No. The boat is well hidden. They will not find it if they look. And I must take supplies tomorrow to Grandfather. It would take too long in the canoe and it wouldn't hold as much."

"I'm afraid, Toby," she said, her face creased with concern. "I don't want anything more to happen to us. I wish you would take the boat back right now."

"No, Lucy!" he said. "It is mine, and I must have it to visit Grandfather."

TWENTY-ONE

Toby was at Monroe Station shortly after dawn. He planned to speak to Bentley about his delay in taking the job, but Big Jim was not there; so he purchased two bags of supplies from Suzie Bentley and then drove back to the camp hurriedly.

He left the camp immediately and made his way to the place on Lost Creek where he had hidden the airboat. After uncovering and loading the boat, he moved cautiously to the edge of the marsh. For several minutes he searched the horizon, making sure that no other airboat was nearby, then he gunned the engine and glided swiftly across the sawgrass, watching constantly for the sight of any moving thing.

The marsh remained as deserted as usual, and Toby ran the airboat at top speed. Soon he approached his grandfather's hammock, but when he made the engine backfire in salute, the old man did not appear on the shore.

Toby left the packages in the boat and walked swiftly along the path. He first sighted the cooking chickee, and there was no fire. This filled him with apprehension, for the fire was never allowed to go out. Then he walked directly to the sleeping chickee.

The old man was lying on the palmetto bed, his eyes closed and his face pale. Toby moved toward him with dread. He lay very still, and flies swarmed around his face.

Toby knelt slowly and touched his grandfather's shoulder. He stirred feebly, and then he looked up. For a moment he said nothing, as if he didn't know who was there, and then he whispered, "Is it Toby?"

"Yes, Grandfather, it is me. I have brought many things, and I'm sorry to have been gone for so long."

"Were you not here only yesterday?"

"No, Grandfather, I was not here. But I will stay now as long as you wish. I will build a fire and then cook food."

The old man waved his hand. "No, Toby. I am not hungry. But I would have coffee. I have not had coffee for many days."

"You will have both," Toby said. "I'll go to the boat and get the supplies, then I will make coffee and a stew. You will be hungry when you smell the pot."

Toby's face was drawn as he went to the boat and brought back the two packages. He knew his grandfather was dying, and his mind was tormented with guilt for having been away for so long.

He started a fire and filled the coffee pot, and then he put a pot of beef stew on the grill. When he went back to the chickee, the old man pushed himself to a sitting position. He then arose slowly and said, "I will sit with you beside the fire."

Toby helped him walk to a palm tree beside the table.

He eased himself to the ground, leaned back against the trunk and said, "The water will soon be gone, Toby. I have seen no fish around the hammock. But I do not seem to be hungry lately. I have made a few cakes of the cornmeal."

Toby said, "Well, you will eat now. I have brought enough to last many days. But you'll not need supplies. You will go back to my camp with me."

The old man's eyes flashed. He said firmly, "No, Toby! I will not do this! I will not leave the marsh! If you take me from here, I will never know peace."

Toby understood. He knew that he himself would have known no peace if he had not brought his son into the marsh. He said, "I will do as you wish, Grandfather. But now you must drink your coffee."

He took the cup eagerly and sipped the hot liquid, seeming to gain strength from Toby's presence. He said, "Do not ever grow old and unneeded, Toby. It is a bad thing to be old and alone. All I have ever known is now no more. Sometimes at night I listen to the thunder of the airplanes passing by, and I think of the days when only the egret and the heron crossed the sky. I am no more a part of this world. It is good that I go now."

"Don't say such things, Grandfather. You're needed by me. And you're going nowhere except to eat stew."

The old man watched as Toby dished up a bowl of broth. He said, "Is it the meat of the deer?"

Toby had forgotten his promise to kill another buck, and he noticed that the pile of firewood and the spit were still beside the chickee. He said, "Yes, Grandfather. It is a very small deer, and the meat seems to be tender."

He put his arm around his grandfather's back and then put the spoon to his mouth.

The old man swallowed, and then he said, "It is good, Toby, and just what I wanted. I thank you, but that is enough. I am not hungry. Maybe I will eat more later." He leaned back against the palm trunk. "How is Lucy?" he asked. "And what of the baby? Will you bring him here when the time comes?"

"She's fine, and I will bring my son here soon. You will teach him much, and he will learn to spear fish and to know the marsh as you know it."

"That is good." The old man suddenly grasped Toby's hand. He said, "There is one thing you must promise me, Toby!"

Toby felt the grip tighten. "What is it, Grandfather?"

"You will take me to the hammock with the others, and I will be with them. There is no one left but you to do this. And you must not take me away from here first. I do not wish to leave the marsh."

Toby said, "You're talking foolish, Grandfather. I will take you to the hammock when the time comes, and I have already said that you will never leave the marsh."

The grip on Toby's hand weakened. His grandfather said, "Toby, do you yet have the ancient medicine bag?"

"Yes, Grandfather, it's at my camp, and I have worn it many times since you gave it to me."

"Use it wisely, Toby, for it is a sacred thing. It will take you to the Great Spirit in the sky. There is a place we will be together again. It is but a short journey. We will soon . . ."

He suddenly slumped forward and was dead.

Toby dropped to his knees and buried his face in his hands, crying unashamedly for a long time, then he picked up his grandfather gently and carried him to the palmetto bed beneath the chickee. He covered him with a blanket, and then he touched the still form and said, "You will not leave the marsh, Grandfather. I'll be back soon to do as I promised. You will rest now, and you will never again be alone."

TWENTY-TWO

As soon as Toby came into the camp, Lucy knew. His face was lined with grief. She said, "He's gone, isn't he?"

"Yes," Toby answered. "He died while I was there. I left him on the hammock because that is what he asked in his last words. There was no food in his chickee, and he wouldn't eat what I prepared. If I hadn't gone there today, he would have died alone."

"I'm sorry," Lucy said. "I should have gone with you to see him more often, but I didn't know he was so ill. I only wish he would have come here and spent his last days with us."

Toby sat at the table and said, "That is not what he wished, Lucy. He was very old, and all that he loved is now gone. He knew only the old ways in the marsh, and that is how he wished his life to end. When he left me there beside the chickee, it was more than the death of an old man, it was the end of a time known only by Grandfather and others before him. There will be no more such as he, and it is now all ended. But it would have been a bad thing for him to die alone."

For a moment Toby became silent, looking back toward the swamp, and then he arose and said, "I will go now to Lowry's sawmill and get planks for the coffin, then I'll go to the Hughes Store and call Josie to come and help. I cannot handle everything alone."

Lucy said, "Should you also call Pappa and ask him to come?"

"No," Toby said quickly. "We will take him to the hammock, and it will be in the old way. You will wear the long dress and also the beads. It will be in the Seminole way, the way of my mother and father and my grandmother. I promised this to Grandfather."

When he returned from the sawmill, Toby sat in the clearing and constructed a crude coffin of cypress planks. It was late afternoon when Josie Billie arrived. Toby immediately said to Lucy, "We'll dress now and then leave for the hammock. I don't want Grandfather to be out there alone."

Toby put on the warrior clothes and the medicine bag and came back outside to wait with Josie. Lucy soon came from the bus wearing the multi-colored long dress. Around her neck there were a dozen strands of glass beads, and she had pulled her long hair into a bun held tight with a hairnet. Josie still wore his usual faded dungarees, but he had on one of the traditional Seminole shirts.

Toby and Josie picked up the coffin, and Lucy followed them down the narrow trail leading through the swamp and to Lost Creek. The sawgrass was undergoing its rainbow change of colors and images as the airboat slowly entered the edge of the marsh. Flights of egrets and herons moved westward into the dim red glow of the day's final light. It would soon be that magical moment when all sound and motion ceases, that brief interlude when day creatures become still and night creatures awaken. Toby and Josie searched the marsh for any sign of other airboats, but there were none.

The airboat cut a steady path through the wall of grass, and soon they approached the hammock. Toby made the engine backfire, and for a moment he expected to look up and see his grandfather standing there on the shore; but the reality of the cypress coffin in the boat told him otherwise.

Lucy went ahead of them and built a fire as Toby and Josie carried the coffin to the chickee. Toby lifted his grandfather and placed him inside, but before he nailed down the top, he placed a carved figure of a deer beside the body.

Lucy made a supper from the supplies Toby had brought that morning, but none of them ate much. Several times Toby left the fire and walked along the dark shore, listening to frogs and searching the night for something that was not there. Sleep came to none of them until close to dawn.

As soon as the first shaft of light cut through the thick caggage palms, Toby and Josie loaded the coffin back into the airboat. Toby gathered all of the pots and dishes and put them into a cloth sack, then he tied his grandfather's old dugout canoe behind the airboat and the procession moved again into the sawgrass.

The hammock was small, not as large as the grandfather's hammock, and it was thickly covered with cabbage palms and dwarf cypress. The edge of the water was lined thickly with button brush, making it necessary for Toby to ram the boat through the foliage to reach the shore.

Once again the coffin was lifted from the airboat, Toby and Josie carrying it inland with Lucy following. They stopped when they entered a small clearing. Placed at random on the ground there were four coffins, three large and one small, and all but the small one were deeply weathered. They placed the new one in the center of the others.

Toby went back to the boat and returned with the cloth sack, a length of rope and a hatchet, then he pulled the cypress canoe into the clearing and placed it beside the coffin. He cut thin cypress poles and tied them with rope, making a frame over the coffin. Then he took a rock, dented all of the pots and threw them on the ground. He smashed the dishes against the edge of the coffin.

For several minutes he stood by the crude box in silence, and then he said, "I'm sorry, Grandfather. I left you alone for too long. You were a good and kind man, and I loved you. There are none left such as you. You will be happy now in the sky, for there are many good things there, and the wind is soft. You are with the others now, and you will never again be alone."

He picked up his grandfather's lancewood spear, snapped it in half and put it on top of the coffin, then he turned to Lucy and said, "It is done. He is where he wished to be. We will go now."

As they started out of the clearing, Toby hesitated for a moment. He grasped the medicine bag tightly, then he looked back at the coffin and said, "I will use it wisely, Grandfather."

TWENTY-THREE

The next morning Toby paced back and forth across the clearing. Several times he went alone into the swamp, and when he returned, he sat at the table in silence. Lucy would speak to him and receive no answer. She knew he was grieving, so she did not try to force herself into his silent and private world.

At noon he refused food, then he got into the pickup and drove away, and it was late afternoon when he returned. He had a thick cardboard box in the back of the truck.

For supper he ate only a few bites of food, and then he went into the bus. When he came back outside he was dressed in the warrior clothes, and the medicine bag hung from his neck. Lucy looked at him quizzically and said, "Why are you wearing those things now? Are you going back to the hammock?"

"I am going to the Osceola Village to see Josie," Toby responded, "and I'll not be gone too long."

It was night when he parked in front of the souvenir store. Children were running around the village chasing each other, and several dogs were fighting over a pile of chicken bones.

Josie and Frank Willie were sitting on the ground beside the chickee, a bottle resting between them. Josie looked up and said, "Hello, Toby. You want a drink? Frank and I are trying to get over the day in the pits."

"I suppose so," Toby said absently, his eyes looking as if he already had too much to drink although he had drunk nothing. Josie noticed this.

Frank Willie got up and said, "I've had enough. I'll go and eat now, and maybe I'll see you later."

Toby sat on the ground and sipped the whiskey. Josie said, "Why are you dressed like that tonight?"

Toby didn't answer. He said instead, "My grandfather didn't weigh even a hundred pounds when he died, and he was once a strong man. There was no food in his chickee, and he said he could no longer find fish. It's the water. Everything will die without water."

Josie said, "It is bad, but maybe we'll get rain soon."

"It is not just that. The white men have turned the water away from the land. I will put it back into the marsh before everything dies just like grandfather."

Josie looked closer at Toby. He said curiously, "And how will you do that?"

"I'll blow a hole in the dike. I have dynamite in the truck that I bought today in Everglades City. Then I will turn water back into the marsh."

Josie shook his head in disbelief of what he was hearing. He said, "Toby, you're not serious, are you? If putting water in the marsh is your purpose, you should as soon stand on the dike and pee. It would do as much good. You would have to fill all the drainage canals and then drop a bomb on the dike at Lake Okeechobee. Then you would get water. But what you say would be only a trickle."

"It would help."

Josie feared for Toby. He said, "Don't do this foolish thing, Toby. You are getting in deeper and deeper. It's not worth it, and sooner or later you're going to get caught. I ask you as my friend, please do not do this thing."

Toby ignored Josie's plea. He said, "Without water, everything out there will die. And the medicine bag will protect me from harm." He got up. "I will see you later. Maybe I'll stop by here on my way back."

Josie watched with anguish as Toby walked from the village.

Five miles east of the village Toby parked the pickup beside the highway. The drainage canal ran parallel to the south side of the road with the dike on the opposite bank.

He put the box on his head and waded into the water, finding that it was no more than chest deep. The long dress clung to his body as he came out on the other side. He took his knife and dug a hole into the side of the dike, then he inserted the dynamite. The fuse was extra long to give him time to go back across the canal and get away, and he hoped it would be enough.

When he finished he climbed to the top of the dike and gazed briefly over the silent marsh, then he went back and put a match to the fuse.

He moved across the water as quickly as possible, and then he ran up the bank to the pickup. He had not noticed the two cars approaching in different directions, and just as he reached the truck, the beaming headlights centered on him. He froze. The light caught in the egret plumes on the turban, causing them to sparkle like fireflies.

Toby had not expected this. He either hesitated too long or the fuse was too short, and suddenly a tremendous boom came out of the darkness. Dirt showered across the highway and onto the top of the pickup, and Toby was knocked flat by the concussion.

One of the cars swerved wildly and then righted itself. It slowed but did not stop. The other was pelted by dirt clods as it sped away from the explosion.

Toby jumped up and scrambled into the truck. Tires screamed as he rammed the accelerator to the floor and raced away into the night. He did not slow the old vehicle as he went past the Osceola Village heading north to his camp.

TWENTY-FOUR

~~~~~~

Toby spent all of the next day carving cypress figures. When he arrived at the camp the night before, Lucy noticed the wet, dirt splattered clothes. She wondered about this but did not question him, and he made no comments as she washed them and hung them on a line beside the chickee to dry.

It was after noon the next day when he put the carvings aside. He looked at Lucy as if finally making a decision. "We have no money left in the camp," he said. "Not even a dollar. Tomorrow I'll go to work for Mr. Bentley. I'll go now and tell him, and maybe tomorrow night I can take the carvings to Josie."

It worried Lucy that he did nothing but sit around the camp in a depressed mood, and this news made her smile. She said, "That's good, Toby. I'm glad this is what you wish to do."

When Toby reached Monroe Station, Bentley was not there. He told Suzie Bentley what he intended, and then he purchased milk, bread and bacon, promising to pay for the items at the end of the week.

Toby noticed the car just before he turned into the camp entrance. It was a green patrol car with a red flasher on top. Lucy was standing by its side, talking to the driver. Fear raced through him like fire in the swamp. He gave the pickup gas and moved past the camp quickly; then two miles down the road he pulled to the rear of a deserted cabin and stopped. Sweat poured from his face, and his hands trembled. As he thought of those days he spent in the jail in Immokalee, he was flooded with a feeling of near panic. It was an hour before he turned the truck and drove back toward the camp.

The patrol car was gone, so he pulled the pickup to the rear of the bus. Lucy came to him immediately. Her voice trembled as she said, "Two men from the sheriff's department were here looking for you. They said they must ask questions. What is this, Toby?"

He did not mention that he had already seen the patrol car at the camp. He asked, "What did you tell them?"

"I only said you were not here. They said they will come again. Is it about the airboat? Do they know?"

"It is more than the airboat," Toby said, his voice hesitant. "I have blown up a dike and done other things. But I don't understand how they could know. If they come again, tell them I'm not here. I must have time to decide what to do."

Before she could speak further, Toby turned and hurried across the clearing and into the woods.

Late that afternoon Josie Billie drove into the camp. Toby was in the edge of the swamp, watching the clearing, and at the sight of the red Mustang he came back to the chickee.

They sat at the table for several minutes with no word spoken, as if some silent understanding was passing between them. Josie's face reflected worry. He finally said, "Toby, there were deputies at the village today asking questions. From things they said, I think they know."

Toby showed no surprise. He said, "Know what?"

"About the airboat and maybe the dike."

"How could they know?"

"I can't answer this, but I think they suspect it was you. Maybe they figure it would be only you who would go past a line of new airboats and then take an old one such as you did."

Lucy was sitting by the grill, listening. With each word her face grew paler.

Josie then asked, "Did anyone see you when you blew the dike?"

"Two cars approached from different directions as I came back to the truck. The fuse was too short, and it blew just as the cars reached my pickup."

"They were asking about the clothes," Josie said. "Have you ever worn them elsewhere?"

Toby thought back to the night when he rammed the knife into the table at Bentley's. He said, "You know I have worn them to your village, and I also wore them once in the store at Monroe Station."

"Damn!" Josie exclaimed. "Why did you wear them when you blew the dike? No one else but you has things like that. Why didn't you just put a neon sign on your back?"

"I didn't think anyone would see."

Josie thought for a moment, and then he said, "Well, that's really no problem. You can hide the clothes in the swamp and there's no way they can prove it was you. You can lie like a white man. Swear you have never been near that dike. And they can prove nothing about the airboat if no one saw you. We'll take it into the marsh and leave it on a hammock, then you will be rid of it."

Toby said, "There is nothing you can do they will not know. They have eyes that see everything except what they don't wish to see."

What Toby said had no meaning to Josie. He said, "I'll come here at noon tomorrow. I have to be at the village in the morning or I'd come sooner. You can take the airboat into the marsh, and I will follow in the canoe. We'll leave it on a hammock and that will be the end of it. There is no way they can prove anything if you admit nothing."

Toby spoke absently, "They are like the hawk flying over the marsh, seeing everything that moves. Even the smallest creature isn't safe from them."

Josie got up and said, "Toby, you're not making sense. Just keep out of sight, and hide the clothes in the swamp as soon as possible. After tomorrow, there will be no need to worry. I will see you at noon."

Toby did not watch as Josie got into the Mustang and drove off. Lucy came to the table and said, "What will you do, Toby?"

"I don't know."

"If you don't wish to do as Josie says, you could go see the deputy and tell him what you've done. Maybe it's not so bad as you think. Mr. Bentley would do all he can to help. And if you do as Josie says, they may never know."

Toby looked across the clearing toward the darkening swamp. His eyes were in deep thought as he said, "Lucy, I have done these things, but not without reason, and now the sky is falling on me. I am being crushed by the white men, just as our people were crushed by them in the past; but I cannot fight them as our people fought. If I fight back I will lose, and that would bring shame and dishonor to the name of my father and my grandfather and those before them. They never lost, but there is no way I can win. If there was I would try. But they will never put me in a cage again. Never! I was born free in the marsh, and I cannot live in a cage."

His words caused Lucy to become even more alarmed. She said, "But you have done nothing so bad, Toby. It is not as you think."

He got up from the table and said, "I will stay in the swamp tonight. If they come again, say I'm not here."

"But you must eat first," she insisted.

"I am not hungry now. I will eat when I return at dawn."

Toby stopped several times as he walked through the swamp, picking leaves from ferns, crushing them in his hands and smelling the sharp fragrance. He watched with interest as squirrels jumped from limb to limb, making their way to their nests for the night. He paused once and let a mother raccoon with her young pass in front of him.

When he reached Lost Creek the light faded, bringing on the silent time. He paused momentarily by his airboat landing where the grass was bare from the many times he had pulled the boat onto the bank. Then he made his way along the path by the creek.

A south wind rustled the sawgrass as he moved instinctively toward the knoll of high land where he had watched the moonrise with Lucy. He sat on the ground and waited, but there was no moon. Ahead of him lay only darkness. He tried to distinguish hammocks from sawgrass but could not do so.

As he sat alone his thoughts drifted from fragment to fragment, dwelling on no one thing but briefly remembering happenings long forgotten and some still vivid — the day he speared his first fish and killed his first deer, smells of food cooking over open fires, the blood on his arm when bitten by a small alligator because he was careless, stripping naked and running through clear water, his first ride on the yellow bus to Everglades City, taunts by white children as he entered school, his fascination when first discovering the crocodiles at Allapattah Flats, vomiting violently after the fire, moving again and again to new hammocks, his first sight of Lucy, walking together into the night, loving beneath the cypress tree, the death cry of a coot suddenly caught in the jaws of allapattah, frustration and anger at the death of the crocodiles, the warden and the judge in Everglades City, pacing back and forth in the jail cell after the airboat suddenly came in front of him, the small coffin, death without reason, the frailness of his grandfather as he placed the lifeless form on the palmetto bed beneath the chickee. He looked into the darkness and all of these things paraded silently through the night. He clutched the ancient medicine bag hanging from his neck, seeking guidance. And then it came to him from the marsh, whispered softly across the somber stretches of endless sawgrass, the last words of his grandfather, *There is a place we will be together again. It is but a short journey.*

TWENTY-FIVE

W hen Toby walked into the clearing at dawn, Lucy had already kindled a fire beneath the grill. She noticed that his face was calm, as if he had just arisen from a deep sleep. She said, "Your breakfast will be ready soon. I have eggs and bacon and an oven of biscuits."

He walked past her and into the bus, and when he came back to the chickee, he was dressed in the warrior clothes. The medicine bag was still around his neck. He sat at the table as she served the food, and then he ate as if very hungry. When he finished he went to the side of the chickee and picked up the frog gig.

Lucy watched each move he made, and she could not understand the sudden change. He no longer had fear or anger in his eyes.

He came back to the table and stood before her, the turban plumes moving gently with a slight breeze. She said, "Are you gigging frogs at this time of day? Always before you have gone only at night."

He spoke calmly and in the manner of his grand-father, pronouncing each word slowly and distinctly, as if reading from an unseen book, "I must leave you now, Lucy. I am going on a journey, but I will see you again soon. I have loved you as I love the marsh and the wind. Know this. But I must go now. There is a place we will be together again. It is but a short journey."

His words and his speech pattern seemed strange to her, but he had spoken and done strange things often during the past few days. She said, "Will you be back by noon? Josie will be here then to help hide the airboat, and he cannot do this alone."

"Tell Josie I need the airboat no longer."

What he said and the way he was speaking brought a sudden horrifying realization to her. She felt the same weakness that overcame her that day he drove from her father's house with the small coffin in the back of the truck. She pleaded, "Toby, do not leave now! Josie will be here at noon, and everything will be fine!"

He took her in his arms and held her gently. "There is no need for you to worry," he said, speaking again in the manner of his grandfather. "I am only going on a journey into the marsh. I will be with you again soon."

He moved away from her quickly and walked across the clearing, the gig gripped in his hand. For a moment she started to run after him as he disappeared into the swamp; and then she repeated the words, "It is not so bad as you think, Toby. Everything will be fine. You must be back by noon."

When he reached Lost Creek, Toby walked past the airboat and to the dugout canoe. He poled the slim craft slowly across the water, and the egrets and herons paid no heed as he moved past them silently. He thought of the times when the airboat engine caused them panic.

He paused for a moment when he reached the beginning of the marsh, looking out over the River of Grass stretching into the distant horizon. He imagined he could see a line of men dressed the same as he, moving swiftly through the sawgrass in canoes, standing erect, their plumes waving with the wind. They circled a small hammock and then turned southward. He looked closer and realized it was only a flight of egrets.

For several minutes he continued to gaze across the vastness of the marsh, then he looked back briefly at the mouth of the creek and pointed the bow of the canoe westward.

Josie arrived at the camp just before noon. As soon as he was out of the car, Lucy ran to him. He noticed immediately the desperate apprehension in her eyes as she said, "He's gone, Josie!"

"Where?" he asked. "Do you know where?"

"I'm not sure, but I think he has gone to Allapattah Flats."

"Did he take the airboat?"

"No. He said to tell you he no longer has need of it."

Josie said urgently, "We must go after him, Lucy! And we must hurry!"

They both ran through the swamp and across the open area of dwarf cypress. When they reached the creek Josie snatched the limbs from the airboat and wired the ignition quickly, then he thundered the boat down the narrow stream and into the edge of the marsh.

Josie's way was blocked by another airboat entering the mouth of the creek. It was a sheriff's patrol with two uniformed men, and they signalled for him to stop. Josie cut the engine as the boat came alongside of him.

One of the deputies said, "Are you Toby Tiger?"

Josie answered, "No, I am Josie Billie. This is Lucy Tiger, Toby's wife. We're looking for Toby."

"So are we. There are questions we must ask him. Is that the boat that was stolen from Gator Sales?"

Josie answered cautiously, "It's Toby's boat, but I don't know that it was stolen. We're only using it to find Toby."

"Do you know where he is?" the deputy asked.

Josie did not want to lead the deputies to Toby, but he felt a desperate urge to find him. He said, "We're not sure, but we think we know."

"You lead and we'll follow."

The two boats shot away across the marsh, the patrol boat running just behind Josie. When they reached the edge of the island, Josie cut the engine and glided the boat onto the shore. The cypress canoe was pulled onto the bank.

They walked single file along the path leading to the back of the cove, Lucy and Josie both moving in fear of what they would find. When they reached the black pool of water Josie steadied Lucy.

The frog gig was rammed into the ground, with the medicine bag tied to its shaft. At its base, the warrior clothes were neatly arranged on the ground. One crocodile lay motionless on the opposite bank, and one was partially out of the water.

As the deputies stared at the long dress and the turban, one said, "That must be the stuff he wore when he blew the dike. They said he had on a dress and a crazy hat. You two wait there while we search the island."

Lucy and Josie remained by the cove as the two men went into the brush in opposite directions. They soon returned, and one of them said, "He's not here. He must have changed clothes to throw us off and then gone on without the canoe, but he can't get far out there in the sawgrass. We'll find him and bring him back. Just leave the airboat on Lost Creek and we'll pick it up later."

As soon as the deputies were gone, Lucy turned to Josie and said, "They'll not find him out there. He is here."

"I know," Josie said. "But do you want me to kill the crocodiles and be sure?"

"No!" Lucy said quickly. "That is not what Toby would wish."

Josie said, "Toby believed it a bad thing to kill without reason, and that is what they have done to him. Only you and I can understand this. But it didn't have to be this way. I tried many times, but he wouldn't listen. He was my friend, and I couldn't help him when he needed me most."

Lucy touched Josie's arm and said, "There was nothing anyone could do. Toby was not of this time, and it would have been best if he had lived in the past, in the days of his grandfather. But that time is gone now forever, and Toby couldn't accept this. I hope he has found what he was seeking." She untied the medicine bag from the gig shaft. "Will you tie a rock to this?" she asked.

Josie found an oblong rock, wound the buckskin thong around it, tied it and handed it back to Lucy. She went down the bank to the edge of the water. For a moment she knelt silently, her arms stretched outward as if reaching for someone not there. Then she threw the rock into the center of the cove. It sank immediately, and her eyes filled with tears as she watched ripples spread across the water.

When she came back to him, Josie said, "What of these things? Do you want the clothes?"

She picked up the strap with the crocodile tooth. "I will keep this," she said, "and we will leave the rest. If he were on the hammock with the others, I would place them on the ground beside him. He would wish for them to be with him now."

Josie said, "I will take you to the reservation, to the house of your mother and father."

"That would be good," Lucy replied. "I cannot stay in the swamp without Toby."

As they started along the path, Lucy stopped and looked back. She said, "Toby . . . Toby . . ." And then she followed Josie to the boat.

Josie pushed the airboat away from the shore. When he connected the ignition wires, the engine thundered to life; then he pushed the throttle forward. For a moment the boat hesitated, and then it shot away rapidly across the endless stretches of somber sawgrass.

f you enjoyed reading this book, here are some other books from Pineapple Press on related topics. To request a catalog or to place an order, visit our website at www.pineapplepress.com. Or write to Pineapple Press, P.O. Box 3889, Sarasota, Florida 34230, or call 1-800-PINEAPL (746-3275).

OTHER BOOKS BY PATRICK SMITH

A Land Remembered. In this best-selling novel, Patrick Smith tells the story of three generations of the MacIveys, a Florida family who battle the hardships of the frontier to rise from a dirt-poor Cracker life to the wealth and standing of real estate tycoons.

Forever Island. A classic novel of the Everglades, *Forever Island* tells the story of Charlie Jumper, a Seminole Indian who clings to the old ways and teaches them to his grandson, even as the white man's world encroaches upon his own.

Angel City. Made into a TV movie, *Angel City* is the powerful and moving exposé of migrant worker camps in Florida in the 1970s.

The River Is Home. Smith's first novel revolves around a Mississippi family's struggle to cope with changes in their rural environment. Poor in material possessions, Skeeter's kinfolk are rich in their appreciation of their beautiful natural surroundings.

A Land Remembered, Student Edition. This best-selling novel is now available to young readers in two volumes. In this edition, the first chapter becomes the last so that the rest of the book is not a flashback. Some of the language and situations have been altered slightly for younger readers.

A Land Remembered Goes to School by Tillie Newhart and Mary Lee Powell. An elementary school teacher's manual, using *A Land Remembered* to teach language arts, social studies, and science, coordinated with the Sunshine State Standards of the Florida Department of Education.

Middle School Teacher Plans and Resources for A Land Remembered: Student Edition by Margaret Paschal. The vocabulary lists, comprehension questions, and post-reading activities for each chapter in the student edition make this teacher's manual a valuable resource. The activities aid in teaching social studies, science, and language arts coordinated with the Sunshine State Standards.

CRACKER WESTERNS
Alligator Gold by Janet Post. On his way home at the end of the Civil War, Caleb Hawkins is focused on getting back to his Florida cattle ranch. But along the way, Hawk encounters a very pregnant Madelaine Wilkes and learns that his only son has gone missing and that his old nemesis, Snake Barber, has taken over his ranch.

Bridger's Run by Jon Wilson. Tom Bridger has come to Florida in 1885 to find his long-lost uncle and a hidden treasure. It all comes down to a boxing match between Tom and the Key West Slasher.

Riders of the Suwannee by Lee Gramling. Tate Barkley returns to 1870s Florida just in time to come to the aid of a young widow and her children as they fight to save their homestead from outlaws.

Ghosts of the Green Swamp by Lee Gramling. Saddle up your easy chair and kick back for a Cracker Western featuring that rough-and-ready but soft-hearted Florida cowboy, Tate Barkley, introduced in *Riders of the Suwannee*.

Guns of the Palmetto Plains by Rick Tonyan. As the Civil War explodes over Florida, Tree Hooker dodges Union soldiers and Florida outlaws to drive cattle to feed the starving Confederacy.

Thunder on the St. Johns by Lee Gramling. Riverboat gambler Chance Ramsay teams up with the family of young Josh Carpenter and the trapper's daughter Abby Macklin to combat a slew of greedy outlaws seeking to destroy the dreams of honest homesteaders.

Trail from St. Augustine by Lee Gramling. A young trapper, a crusty ex-sailor, and an indentured servant girl fleeing a cruel master join forces to cross the Florida wilderness in search of buried treasure and a new life.

Wiregrass Country by Herb and Muncy Chapman. Set in 1835, this historical novel will transport you to a time when Florida settlers were few and laws were scarce. Meet the Dovers, a family of homesteaders determined to survive against all odds and triumph against the daily struggles that accompany running a cattle ranch.

FLORIDA HISTORY

Old Florida Style: A Story of Cracker Cattle (DVD) by Steve Kidd and Alex Menendez, Delve Productions. This DVD showcases Florida's Cracker heritage. Saddle up a tough little Cracker horse called a marsh tacky and explore old Florida—when cow hunters pulled the rugged Spanish cattle out of the palmettos and established this as a cattle state.

Time Traveler's Guide to Florida by Jack Powell. A unique guidebook that describes 70 places and reenactments in Florida where you can experience the past, and a few where you can time-travel into the future.

Florida's Past: People and Events that Shaped the State by Gene Burnett. The three volumes in this series are chock-full of carefully researched, eclectic essays written in Gene Burnett's easygoing style. Many of these essays on Florida history were originally published in *Florida Trend* magazine.

Tropical Surge by Benjamin Reilly. This engaging historical narrative covers many significant events in the history of south Florida, including the major developments and setbacks in the early years of Miami and Key West, as well as an in-depth look at Henry Flagler's amazing Overseas Railway.

OTHER FICTION

Adventures in Nowhere by John Ames. A boy in 1950s Florida wrestles with adult problems and enjoys the last days of his boyhood in a place called Nowhere, sometimes fearing for his sanity as his family falls apart and he watches a house change shape across the river.

Seven Mile Bridge by Michael Biehl. Florida Keys dive shop owner Jonathan Bruckner returns home to Sheboygan, Wisconsin, after his mother's death. What he finds leads him to an understanding of the mystery that surrounded his father's death years before.

The Bucket Flower by Donald Robert Wilson. In 1893, 23-year-old Elizabeth Sprague goes into the Everglades to study its unique plant life, even though she's warned that a pampered "bucket flower" like her can't endure the rigors of the swamp. She encounters wild animals and even wilder men but finds her own strength and a new future.

My Brother Michael by Janis Owens. Out of the shotgun houses and deep, shaded porches of a West Florida mill town comes this extraordinary novel of love and redemption. Gabriel Catts recounts his lifelong love for his brother's wife, Myra—whose own demons threaten to overwhelm all three of them.

Black Creek by Paul Varnes. Through the story of one family, we learn how white settlers moved into the Florida territory, taking it from the natives—who had been here only a few generations—with false treaties and finally all-out war. Thus, both sides were newcomers anxious to "take Florida."

Confederate Money by Paul Varnes. In 1861, as this novel opens, a Confederate dollar is worth 90 cents. We follow Henry Fern as he fights on both sides of the war. Through shrewd dealings, he manages to amass $40,000 in Confederate paper money and finally changes his paper fortune into silver and gold.

For God, Gold and Glory by E. H. Haines. The riveting account of the invasion of the American Southeast from 1539 to 1543 by Hernando de Soto, as told by his private secretary, Rodrigo Ranjel. A meticulously researched tale of adventure and survival and the dark aspects of greed and power.

Nobody's Hero by Frank Laumer. Based on the true adventure of an American soldier who refused to die in spite of terrible wounds sustained during the battle known as Dade's Massacre, which started the Second Seminole War in Florida.

THE HONOR SERIES

"Sign on early and set sail with Peter Wake for both solid historical context and exciting sea stories." —U.S. Naval Institute Proceedings

The Honor Series of naval fiction by Robert N. Macomber. Covers the life and career of American naval officer Peter Wake from 1863 to 1907. The first book in the series, *At the Point of Honor,* won Best Historical Novel from the Florida Historical Society. The second, *Point of Honor,* won the Cook Literary Award for Best Work in Southern Fiction. The sixth, *A Different Kind of Honor,* won the Boyd Literary Award for Excellence in Military Fiction from the American Library Association.

CPSIA information can be obtained at www.ICGtesting.com
Printed in the USA
BVOW070819020413

317014BV00002B/3/P